For a Night of Love

Emile Zola

Translated by Andrew Brown

ET REMOTISSIMA PROPE

100 PAGES

100 PAGES

Published by Hesperus Press Limited
4 Rickett Street, London sw6 1ru
www.hesperuspress.com

For a Night of Love first published in French as *Pour une nuit d'amour* in 1876;
Nantas first published in French in 1878; *Fasting* first published in French as
Le Jeûne in 1870
This translation first published by Hesperus Press Limited, 2002
Reprinted 2003

Introduction and English language translation © Andrew Brown, 2002
Foreword © A.N. Wilson, 2002

Designed and typeset by Fraser Muggeridge
Printed in the United Arab Emirates by Oriental Press

ISBN: 1-84391-010-1

CONTENTS

Writing to his friend Thomas Sergeant Perry, of Rhode Island, Henry James said, 'I heard Zola characterises his manner sometime since as *merde à la vanille*. I send you by post Zola's last – *merde au naturel*. Simply hideous.' It is, for the master of circumlocution, a somewhat startling joke, but it conveys Zola's shock value. James's letter was written in 1876; the Zola novel in question was *Son Excellence Eugène Rougon*. We only have to recall the climate of opinion over the Channel in London to imagine how startlingly frank Zola must have seemed to his contemporaries. In 1891, the publisher Macmillan asked Thomas Hardy to tone down a scene in *Tess of the D'Urbevilles* in which Angel Clare picks up the heroine in his arms and carries her over a ford. In the published version, to spare the blushes of readers, Tess is trundled over the stream in a wheelbarrow.

Zola, meanwhile, had written a whole series of novels in which the sexual needs of his female characters were fully explored. One thinks of the striptease artiste Nana and her string of hireling lovers; or the womenfolk of the miners in *Germinal*, all freely indulging in sexual activity and displayed to the reader in the full realism of their energy and appetite. Or think of the girls who sell charcuterie in *Le Ventre de Paris*. The men they fancy, mock, and enjoy are seen as no more or less than the bits of meat they handle all day long in their market stalls in Les Halles.

We can't doubt that Zola depicted the world with punctilious accuracy. He is the master of detail piled upon detail. His novels and tales achieve their effect by thoroughly researched reportage. Whether he is describing the working routines of a coal-miner, or a laundress, or a clerk, or a priest, he takes you through every detail of what they do, from their waking moment to sleep again.

To enjoy Zola at his best, therefore, you have to read one of the great novels, in which a whole panorama emerges, as in the work of one of those highly realistic nineteenth-century painters, such as William Powell Frith (1818–1909), who attended to every last bootstrap or railway ticket clutched in the hands of characters who swarm across his canvases. Even in these shorter works, however, you can catch the flavour of Zola's brilliance.

Henry James would no doubt have applied the scatological metaphor to the longest of the stories in this collection, 'For a Night of Love'. It is a neat plot, ideally suited to its length, and with three main protagonists. Thérèse is a beautiful young woman in a small provincial town. Through the eyes of a gangling, awkward clerk, Julien, we enjoy ogling at her, glimpsing her from afar, deriving excessive sexual excitement from the glimpse of her letting her hair down as her maid undresses her for the night. He tries to woo her by playing the flute, a rather obviously phallic instrument, and seethes with fury when he realises that he has a rival.

Thérèse is a sadist, which adds to the kinky charm of the story. She has always enjoyed tormenting Colombel, a young man with whom, as a baby, she had shared a wet-nurse. Their love affair, when it develops, has almost something of incest about it. And their lovemaking is violent, including much wrestling and the exchange of insults. Again, think of the characters in English novels of this period, or even the characters in the urbane and sophisticated novels of James! We might enjoy guessing what Dorothea and Mr Casaubon got up to in the bedroom in *Middlemarch*, but we are certainly never told by George Eliot.

Thérèse kills Colombel during one of their violent romps. She offers Julien a night of love if he will dispose of the corpse. The actual business of his taking the body to the bridge and dumping it in the water is as exciting and full of suspense as a Patricia Highsmith story. (One wonders whether Highsmith knew this tale, in fact.) Julien's reveries, however, are distinctively late nineteenth-century ones. His carnal imaginings about Thérèse in a state of undress turn into a sick yearning for death. *Liebestod* in the French provincial manner follows. The morning light shows not Julien and Thérèse twisted in the bedroom sheets, but Julien and Colombel at the bottom of the river.

The high camp of 'Fasting' is very different in atmosphere. Zola had a line in highly anti-clerical tales that bordered on the pornographic. In one of these, *La Faute de l'Abbé Mouret*, we watch a young priest being seduced by a sort of gypsy earth maiden in naked garden scenes worthy of D.H. Lawrence. In 'Fasting' the erotic undertones of the relationship between the pampered curate and his silly aristocratic female congregation are much more subdued.

> 'While from up in his pulpit he was talking of bones cracking and limbs roasting, the little Baroness, half asleep as she was, saw him at her table, blissfully wiping his lips, telling her, "My dear madame, this is a bisque which would ensure you found grace in the sight of God the Father, if your beauty were not already sufficient for you to be certain of a place in paradise."'

The unmistakable point of the story is that Catholicism, indeed all religion, can never give true sustenance to the human spirit. Anyone who looks to religion to be nourished, like the hungry sheep in Milton's *Lycidas*, will be unfed.

In 'Nantas' we find ourselves in the world in which Zola's imagination really felt most at home, the crowded Paris of the 1870s, its rain-soaked streets, its garrets where young people, lured to the big city from the provinces, lie hungry in the intervals of their tedious work and emotionally unfulfilled lives. Nantas believes himself to have one asset – his 'strength'. He has paced the streets of Paris, and found nothing; he is down to his last hunk of bread when the offer comes. Thereafter, Nantas' meteoric rise to a ministerial post is not really very plausible. Balzac could have made it so. The core of the story, though, is not so much the outward 'success' of Nantas' life as his inner perceptions of himself and his sexual needs. Hence, the power of its closing scene with Nantas attempting to blow his brains out, and Flavie at the last minute bursting into the room to say she loves him. After humiliating him with a sexless marriage, she has at last sniffed *strength*. We are back in Zola country.

– *A.N. Wilson, 2002*

Two of these stories are about the way contracts between men and women unexpectedly break down. In 'For a Night of Love', Thérèse de Marsanne kills her lover Colombel in a sado-masochistic tussle. Knowing that Julien Michon is in love with her (he has shyly been serenading her from a neighbouring house with his flute), she beckons him over, and offers him a deal: if he will dispose of her lover's body, she will give herself to him. In 'Nantas', the contract is between Nantas on the one side, and Flavie Danvilliers on the other. She has not murdered her lover, but, with almost equally grave potential repercussions for her family honour, has become pregnant by her momentary paramour, M. des Fondettes, who is already married. This time the deal involves him marrying Flavie in exchange for her rich dowry, which will act as seed capital for him to realise his intentions. Flavie herself insists, as part of the contract, that theirs is to be a *mariage blanc*, with separate lives. At first Nantas is only too happy to accept, so as to devote himself to his financial and political enterprises. But again the contract fails, and again it fails without either of the characters really defaulting on it. Or rather, Nantas does default – but by falling in love with his wife. This leads him to become jealous of her (something he attempts to rationalise by seeing her 'infidelity' as a potential slur on his honour), convincing himself, especially thanks to the machinations of the double-dealing maid, Mlle Chuin, that she has taken up again with M. des Fondettes (who does indeed long to 'possess' her once more). Nantas wants to revoke her autonomy, but in a battle of wills between them realises he cannot, and, broken, retreats, telling her 'you are free'. His political moment of triumph (he has been appointed finance minister by Napoleon III) has been rendered worthless: he will put the finishing touches to his budget and then kill himself.

Contracts are particularly fragile when, as in these two cases, they involve sex: their vulnerability is increased by the fact that the signatories to the bargain are not social equals. In both these stories, an upper-class woman in a crisis offers a deal to a lower-class man who needs her (for her love or her money). In 'For a Night of Love', Thérèse requires Julien's physical strength to dispose of Colombel's body; Julien successfully performs his task, and thereby gains a right to the woman's body, and thus to sexuality (he is a virgin): but he ends up refusing it, and life itself. In 'Nantas', Flavie needs Nantas' 'name' to legitimise her child (who then conveniently disappears from the story), and allow her to remain part of the Danvilliers clan. Nantas keeps his side of the bargain, and gains a fortune that opens up his path to political power (his success is partly due to the sublimation of energies that are not channelled into a full marital relationship). His 'strength' is a leitmotif of the story: it is not simple physical strength, like Julien's, but the strength of will and intellect that enable him, even on the evening he is plotting to murder both his wife and her assumed lover, to show such eloquence at dinner on the subject of his projected budget that his daring new financial plans even convince his more conservative father-in-law. Nantas himself is by now convinced that his strength is worthless, since it has not gained him his wife's love – but even as he privately decides that, although he has won everything, without her he has nothing, we see Flavie viewing him with an enigmatic new tenderness. And just as he is about to shoot himself (in the same Parisian garret where he had spent two penniless months trying to find a job – both 'Nantas' and 'For a Night of Love' are topographically circular), Flavie bursts in to declare that she does now love him because he is – in the story's last word – 'strong'. The aphrodisiac of power seems to have worked its charm. And yet the melodramatic coincidences that Zola foregrounds (it is just as Nantas is going to kill himself first time round that Mlle Chuin is shown in, like a fairy godmother, to wave her wand and offer him a rich marriage; it is just as he is going to blow his brains out that Flavie rushes in to pronounce the equally magical words 'je t'aime') suggest that Nantas' 'strength' is only part of the story. On both occasions, it has not been enough by itself to save him: he needs help from outside, from a woman. Any strength he has must be *recognised* (by Mlle Chuin in the first instance, by Flavie in the second) for it to be effective. Without this recognition, he will die – yet another victim of a Paris depicted, in the early scenes, as tantalising in its Second-Empire bustle and glamour but also as inhuman and anonymous. Flavie's final gift of herself is a sublation of the original contract, which as a *mariage blanc* was a paradox (or a compromise): now that their relation is to be a proper marriage, the separation accepted as part of the original terms is annulled.

Both Thérèse and Flavie are haughty and imperious *femmes fatales*, simultaneously subversive and conformist. They are subversive in challenging the traditional roles of women, but conformist in that they both ultimately uphold the established order: Thérèse allows Julien to be her scapegoat for Colombel's death, and having thus eliminated two plebeian suitors marries a member of her own aristocratic caste; Flavie falls in love with Nantas because he has shown himself an adroit financial and political manipulator – her love is given only for a specific reason ('because you are strong') and thus tacitly imposes another condition: that his strength should continue. We may legitimately fear for the couple's newly romantic relationship if a ministerial reshuffle precipitates Nantas from his eminence, just as Thérèse is unlikely to be satisfied by the young Comte de Véteuil unless, like Colombel, he is prepared to give her a bit of rough stuff.

These contractual aspects of the two stories act as a narrative scheme around which Zola weaves a web of impressionistic evocations. These are limited in 'Nantas' to the brief vignettes of the streets of Paris or the chime of the cash registers in Nantas' firm: in 'For a Night of Love', they are more poetic. Thérèse is a white-faced, black-eyed, red-lipped frost-queen from an Edvard Munch canvas. Her haughty exterior conceals a baroque passion; she lives in a house that is compared to both a tomb and a church, and she bears the name of a saint (Teresa of Avila) closely associated with the intersection between fleshly and spiritual love (Thérèse herself is a mixture of intense piety and eroticism). The taciturn Julien finds absorption in a lyrical, ever-constant nature, and his only mode of self-expression is through that most natural instrument, a wooden flute. This is a story of chiaroscuro effects being disturbed by the harsher edges of black and white. Julien's dark nocturne is slashed open by the dazzling light from Thérèse's room, his grey placidity intruded on by the whiteness of her face and dress. His music should be heard, not seen – it initially attracts Thérèse, but then she sees the ugly young man playing it. His final refusal to take advantage of her offer marks a turn back from her 'culture' (the aristocratic residence, the elegant young men, the noisy waltzes, the underlying cruelty) to his 'nature', associated with music (the river Chanteclair with its clear song), the tranquillity of nature, and identification with his rival (almost his double) Colombel, calling him home to death.

'Fasting', in its depiction of a gourmet curate who preaches ascetic self-denial to a congregation of pampered upper-class women, is very different from the other two tales in this collection. Obviously anti-clerical in tone, on a deeper level it engages with the sheer sensuality of Catholicism that proved such an ambiguous source of attraction to the 'decadent' movement of the fin-de-siècle. The Baroness listening drowsily to the sermon is enveloped in a warm bath of mildly erotic fervour, and responds to the *sound* of the curate's words, not to their *sense* – 'as some to church repair, / Not for the doctrine, but the music there' (Pope, *An Essay on Criticism*). This is a story of hot air: the Baroness swoons at the 'music' of the curate's vacuous rhetoric, but even more at the warm gusts from the air vent playing up her skirt (the French 'bouche de chaleur', 'mouth of warmth', is nicely explicit). It is also a story which, like James Joyce in the 'Lotus-Eaters' episode of *Ulysses* (communion as the injunction to 'shut your eyes and open your mouth' for the 'lollipop' of the host), focuses on the intensely oral aspects of Catholicism: the curate's words, preaching mortification, come from the same mouth whose 'ready tongue' wags in the salons of his 'magdalens', and absorbs the Baroness' salmon pâté and Pommard with the fervour of someone taking the bread and the wine. The title, 'Fasting', is doubly ironic. This church is failing to provide its congregation with the real bread of angels: full bodily communion is replaced by mere fantasies – vaguely idealistic, languidly erotic products of sublimation. In this kind of society, even the well-fed little Baroness is left, in a real sense, fasting: hungry for something more real than the twilit boudoir of the church. And, though the text necessarily cannot say this, history is soon to impose its own fasting on a society indifferent to the unchosen ascesis, the hungers of every kind sapping the strength of the Second Empire. The story was published in early 1870: some of its first readers would before long be part of the starving population of a Paris besieged by the Prussian army and torn apart by civil war and revolution, lucky to dine, not off salmon pâté, but dogs and rats.

– Andrew Brown, 2002

Note on Publication Dates:
'Fasting' ('Le Jeûne'), was published in March 1870. In June of that year, the first volume (*La Fortune des Rougon*) of Zola's massive sequence of novels on life under the Second Empire, *Les Rougon-Macquart*, started serialisation. 'For a Night of Love' ('Pour une nuit d'amour') was written for the Russian review, *Le Messager de l'Europe*, where it was published in 1876. It was also published in the French review *L'Echo universel* in 1877. 'Nantas' too was published in *Le Messager de l'Europe*, in October 1878 – this being contemporary with the composition of the first chapters of *Nana*, Zola's study of the Parisian *demi-monde* under the Second Empire (eventually published in 1880): but its storyline has more in common with another instalment of the *Rougon-Macquart* series, *La Curée* (*The Kill*), published in 1871.

For a Night of Love[*]

[*] [Zola's Note]: The first idea for this novella came from Casanova.

The small town of P*** is built on a hill. At the foot of the ancient ramparts flows a very deep stream with steep banks, the Chanteclair, doubtless so called because of the crystal-clear song of its limpid water. Arriving along the road from Versailles, the traveller first crosses the Chanteclair over the single span of the stone bridge to the south gate of the town: the bridge's broad parapets, low and rounded, are used as benches by all the old men of the district. Opposite, the rue Beau-Soleil leads up to a silent square, the Place des Quatre-Femmes, paved with rough slabs of stone, and overrun with thick grass, which makes it look as green as a meadow. The houses sleep. Every half hour, the footsteps of some passer-by dawdling along set a dog barking behind a stable door; and the one bit of excitement in this isolated spot is still the officers heading off, twice a day at their regular time, for a meal at their guest-house in the rue Beau-Soleil.

It was in a gardener's house, on the left, that Julien Michon lived. The gardener had rented out to him a big first-floor room; and, as the gardener himself lived on the other side of the house, looking out onto the rue Catherine where his garden was, Julien lived there in peace and quiet, with his own staircase and door, already content, at the age of twenty-five, to follow the set routines of a reclusive petit bourgeois.

The young man had lost his mother and father very early on in life. The Michons had, in days gone by, been saddlers at Les Alluets, near Mantes. On their death, an uncle had sent the child off to boarding school. Then the uncle himself had passed away, and for five years Julien had had a little job as a copying clerk in the P*** post office. He earned fifteen hundred francs, without a hope of ever earning more. In any case, he saved his money, and couldn't imagine a more comfortable or a happier condition than his own.

Tall, strong, and bony, Julien had big hands that got in his way. He felt he was ugly, with a square head that looked as if it had been left unfinished after some rough handling by a sculptor all fingers and thumbs; and this made him shy, especially in the presence of young ladies. When a laundress had told him with a laugh that he wasn't so bad looking, it had left him feeling deeply disturbed. When he ventured out, his arms dangling, his shoulders hunched, his head hanging low, he would take long loping strides to return more quickly into his shadow. His clumsiness left him prey to a continual sense of fright, a pathological longing for ordinariness and obscurity. He seemed to have resigned himself to growing old in this way, without friendship, without love affairs, with the tastes of a cloistered monk.

And this life did not weigh heavily on his broad shoulders. Julien, at heart, was very happy. He had a calm and transparent soul. His daily life, dominated by fixed rules, was imbued with serenity. In the morning he would go to his office, and placidly take up his work where he had left off the night before; then, he would have a bread roll for lunch, and continue his writing; then he had dinner, went to bed, slept. The next day, the sun would rise on the same schedule, week by week, month by month. This slow procession came to be accompanied by a soft and gentle music, rocking him in the daydream of those oxen that pull the cart along and then spend the evening ruminating among fresh straw. He drank in all the charm of monotony. Sometimes, after dinner, he would enjoy going down the rue Beau-Soleil, and sitting on the bridge, waiting for nine o'clock. He let his legs dangle over the water, watching the Chanteclair flowing along beneath him, with the pure murmur of its silver waves. Willows, along both

4

river-banks, trailed their pale heads in their own reflections. From the sky drifted down the fine ashen hues of dusk. And there he would remain, in the midst of this great calm, held in its charm and reflecting vaguely that the Chanteclair must be as happy as he was, gliding continually over the same water-weeds, in such a pleasant silence. When the stars came out, he would go home to bed, his lungs filled with freshness.

These weren't by any means the only pleasures Julien indulged in. On his days off, he would set out on foot by himself, happily walking for miles and coming back exhausted. He had also made friends with a mute wood-carver: arm in arm they would stroll up and down the riverside walk for entire afternoons, without even exchanging a sign. At other times, ensconced in the back of the Café des Voyageurs, he and the mute would get stuck into interminable games of draughts, punctuated by long periods of immobility while they planned their moves. He had once had a dog that had got run over by a carriage, and he remembered him with such religious devotion that he didn't want any more pets. At the post office, they teased him about a kid girl, a ten-year-old, barefooted raga-muffin who sold boxes of matches: he would give her a big handful of coins without buying any of her wares; but he was cross at being noticed and made sure no one was watching when he slipped her the money. He was never seen out, of an evening, with some piece of skirt on the ramparts. The working girls of P***, streetwise lasses with nothing to learn about life, had themselves ended up leaving him alone, seeing him choked with shyness in their presence, convinced as he was that their friendly come-hitherish laughter was really mockery. Some of the townspeople said he was stupid, others maintained that you had to watch boys like that, the quiet ones, the loners.

5

Julien's paradise, the place where he could breathe easily, was his room. Only there did he feel safe from the world. There he could stand tall, laugh to himself; and, when he caught sight of his reflection in the mirror, he couldn't get over his surprise at how young he looked. The room was huge; he had furnished it with a big settee, and a round table with two upright chairs and an armchair. But this still left room for him to walk about: the bed was set well back in the recesses of a deep alcove; a small walnut chest of drawers, between the two windows, seemed no bigger than a child's toy. He would pace up and down, stretching his legs, never tiring of his own company. He never wrote, outside his office hours, and reading tired him. As the old woman who kept the guesthouse where he ate insisted on trying to educate him by lending him novels, he would bring them back to her, unable to say what was in them: such complicated stories were in his view entirely lacking in common sense. He drew a little, always the same head, a woman in profile, severe of aspect, with broad headbands and a string of pearls in her chignon. His sole passion was music. For entire evenings, he would play the flute, and this, more than anything, was his main way of relaxing.

Julien had taught himself the flute. For a long time, an old flute in yellow wood that he saw in a junk shop on the Place du Marché had been the object of some of his most intense longings. He had the money: it was just that he didn't dare go in and buy it, for fear of looking ridiculous. Finally, one evening, he had plucked up enough courage to run off with the flute hidden under his jacket, hugged tight to his chest. Then, having closed his doors and windows, very softly so no one would hear, he had spent two years fingering his way through an old flute manual he came across in a little bookshop.

Only in the last six months had he risked playing it with his windows open. He knew only old, slow, simple tunes, eighteenth-century romances, that were filled with infinite tenderness when he stuttered them out with the faltering breath of an over-emotional pupil. On warm evenings, when everyone in the neighbourhood was asleep, and this delicate melody wafted out from the big room lit by one candle, it sounded like the voice of someone in love, tremulous and low, confiding to solitude and night what it would never have dared say to the light of day.

Often, indeed, as he knew the tunes by heart, Julien would blow out the candle, to save expenses. In any case, he liked the shadows. Then, sitting at the window, looking out at the sky, he would play in the dark. People going by would look up to see where this music was coming from, so frail and so beautiful, like the distant trills of a nightingale. The old flute in yellow wood was slightly cracked, which gave it a veiled sound, a delightfully reedy voice like that of a marquise of bygone times, still singing in the purest tones the minuets of her youth. One by one the notes would fly away, gently rustling their wings. It seemed that the song was being sung by Night herself, so closely did it mingle with the discreet breezes in the darkness.

Julien lived in fear that people in the neighbourhood might complain. But they are heavy sleepers out in the provinces. In any case, there were only two residents living in the Place des Quatre-Femmes: a lawyer, M. Savournin, and an old retired gendarme, Captain Pidoux, both of them no trouble as neighbours, in bed and asleep by nine. Julien was more worried about the people who lived in the noble dwelling known as the Hôtel de Marsanne, which rose on the other side of the square, its grey and gloomy façade as grim as a monastery's, right opposite his windows. Five grass-grown steps led up to a round-arched front door, defended by enormous nail-heads. Ten window casements stretched along the house's single upper floor, and their shutters opened and closed at the same times every day, without letting anyone see into the rooms, sheltered behind the thick curtains that were always closed. On the left, the tall chestnut trees in the garden formed a clump of greenery, its leaves swelling up to the ramparts. And this imposing town house, with its grounds, its sombre walls, its atmosphere of royal boredom, made Julien reflect that if the Marsanne family didn't like the flute, they need certainly only say the word, and he would have to stop playing.

Moreover, the young man felt a sense of religious awe when he leaned out of his window and gazed at the vast extent of the garden and the buildings. The house was famous in this part of the world, and it was said that strangers came from miles around to visit it. And the wealth of the Marsannes was swathed in legend. For a long time, Julien had watched the ancient house, trying to fathom the mysteries of the all-powerful fortune it concealed. But in all the hours he spent there in absorbed contemplation, he never saw anything but the grey façade and the black clump of the chestnut trees. Never once did he see a soul go up the loose, wobbly steps, never once did the front door, green with moss, open. The Marsannes had blocked it up, the entrance was through an iron gate on the rue Sainte-Anne; in addition, at the far end of a narrow street, near the ramparts, there was a little gate onto the garden, which Julien couldn't see. For him, the house remained dead, like one of those palaces in fairy tales, peopled with invisible inhabitants. Every morning and every evening, all he ever saw were the arms of the servant pushing open or

8

closing the shutters. Then, the house would reassume its intensely melancholy feel of some abandoned tomb in the stillness of a cemetery. The foliage of the chestnut trees was so thick that their branches concealed the garden paths. And this hermetically sealed existence, haughty and silent, made the young man's heart beat twice as fast. So this was wealth, was it? – this gloomy tranquillity, in which he recognised the same religious shudder that befalls anyone gazing up at the vaulting of churches.

How often, before going to bed, had he blown out his candle and stood for an hour at his window, trying to pierce the secrets of the Marsanne family house! At night, it stood out in a dark mass against the sky, and the chestnut trees spread out in a pool of inky darkness. The people inside must have drawn the curtains tightly closed, since not a gleam of light escaped between the slats of the shutters. The house didn't even have that lived-in atmosphere of a place where you can sense people breathing in their sleep. It vanished into nothing in the darkness. It was at such times that Julien plucked up courage and picked up his flute. He could play with impunity; his rippling little notes echoed back from the empty house; some of his slower phrases melted into the garden shadows where not even the flapping of a bird's wings could be heard. The old yellow-wood flute seemed to be playing its ancient tunes outside the castle of the Sleeping Beauty.

One Sunday, on the Place de l'Eglise, one of the postal workers abruptly pointed out to Julien a tall old man and an elderly lady, and told him their names. It was the Marquis and Marquise de Marsanne. They went out so rarely that he had never seen them before. He was overwhelmed at the sight of their pinched, solemn frames, walking along at a measured pace, greeted by deep bows and replying with the merest nod.

Then, Julien's friend informed him in rapid succession that they had a daughter still at convent school, Mlle Thérèse de Marsanne, and that young Colombel, the clerk of M. Savournin the lawyer, had been suckled by the same wet-nurse. And indeed, as the two elderly people were turning into the rue Sainte-Anne, young Colombel, who was just passing, went up, and the Marquis proffered him his hand, an honour he had shown no one else. Julien was jealous at this hand-shake, for this Colombel, a youth of twenty, bright-eyed and mean-mouthed, had been his enemy for a long time. He teased Julien for his timidity, and set all the washerwomen of the rue Beau-Soleil against him – with the result that one day, on the ramparts, they had challenged each other to a fist-fight, from which the lawyer's clerk had emerged with two black eyes. And the evening he found out these new details, Julien played his flute even more softly.

Yet he did not allow his obsession with the Marsanne house to disturb his habits, still as regular as clockwork. He continued to go to his office, to have lunch and dinner, to go for his usual walk by the Chanteclair. The house itself, with its vast peacefulness, finally became one more part of his life's even tenor. Two years went by. He was so used to the sight of the grass growing on the steps, the grey façade, the black shutters, that these things seemed to him to be definitive, necessary to the slumber of the neighbourhood.

Julien had been living on the Place des Quatre-Femmes for five years when, one July evening, an event turned his life upside down. The night was very warm and lit with bright stars. He was playing his flute in the dark, but absent-mindedly, slowing down and almost dozing off at certain notes, when suddenly, right opposite, a window of the Marsanne house opened, a slash of brilliant light in the dark façade. A young girl had come to lean out, and remained at the window: he could see her slender outline, she seemed to be looking across, lending an attentive ear. Julien, trembling, had stopped playing. He couldn't make out the girl's face, he could see only her flowing hair, already let down round her neck. And a light voice came to him through the silence.

'Didn't you hear that, Françoise? It sounded like music.'

'It must be a nightingale, mademoiselle,' replied a rough voice from within. 'Close the shutters, don't let in the night creatures.'

Once the façade had become black once more, Julien was unable to leave his armchair, his eyes still dazzled by the gash of light in the wall that up until then had been dead. And he couldn't stop shaking, wondering if he should be pleased at this apparition. Then, an hour later, he resumed his quiet flute-playing. The thought that the young girl doubtless imagined there was a nightingale in the chestnut trees made him smile.

2

Next day, at the post office, the latest news was that Mlle Thérèse de Marsanne had just left her convent school. Julien told no one he had seen her with her hair down and her neck bare. He was in a state of great disquiet; he felt an indefinable hostility towards this young girl, who was going to upset his habits. Certainly, that window would annoy him terribly: he would dread seeing its shutters opening at all hours. He would no longer feel at home, he would even have preferred a man than a woman to live opposite, since women are more prone to make fun. How would he find the courage to play his flute now? He played too badly to please a lady who was bound to know about music. So, that evening, after turning it over and over in his mind, he was sure he hated Thérèse.

Julien returned home furtively. He didn't light a candle. That way, she wouldn't see him. He wanted to go to bed straight away, to show what a bad mood he was in. But he couldn't resist the need to know what was going on opposite. The window didn't open. Only around ten o'clock did a pale light finally gleam between the slats of the shutters; then the gleam was extinguished, and he was left gazing at the dark window. From then on, every evening, he resumed this espionage, in spite of himself. He kept the house under surveillance; as he had at first, he strained every nerve to pick up the tiniest tremors that gave life to its old mute stones. Nothing seemed changed, the house continued to sleep its deep sleep; you needed expert ears and eyes to catch a hint of the new life there. Sometimes, there was a flicker of light moving behind the windows, the corner of a curtain was lifted, giving him a glimpse into a huge room. At other times, light footsteps could be heard crossing the garden, the distant sound of a piano reached him, accompanying a voice singing; or the sounds remained even vaguer, a simple passing ripple pointing to the beating of a young heart in the old dwelling. Julien explained his curiosity to himself as the result of his great irritation at all this noise. How he missed the time when the empty house echoed back the subdued sound of his flute!

One of his most avid desires, though he wouldn't admit it to himself, was to see Thérèse again. He imagined her in his mind's eye, pink-faced, mocking, her eyes gleaming. But as he never ventured to his window in daylight, he caught a glimpse of her only at night, when she was swallowed up in the grey shadows. One morning, as he was closing one of his shutters to keep the sun out, he caught sight of Thérèse standing in the middle of her room. He remained rooted to the spot, not daring to move a muscle. She seemed to be thinking something over, she was very tall, very pale, her face classically beautiful. And he felt almost intimidated by her, she was so different from the light-hearted image he had formed of her. Especially noticeable was her mouth, rather large with bright-red lips, and deep eyes, dark and lustreless, which gave her the appearance of a cruel queen. Slowly, she came over to the window; but she didn't seem to see him, as if he were too far off, too indistinct. She moved away, and the swing of her head was so powerful in its grace that he felt weaker than a child in comparison with her, for all his broad shoulders. When he got to know her, he feared her all the more.

Thus began for the young man a wretched existence. This beautiful young lady, so grave and noble, who lived near him, drove him to despair. She never looked at him, she was unaware of his existence. But this did not stop his heart quailing at the thought that she might notice him and find him ridiculous. His pathological shyness made him think that she was spying on his every move so as to make fun of him. He would scurry home with his tail between his legs, and in his room he avoided moving about. Then, after a month, he started to suffer from the girl's disdain. Why didn't she ever look at him? She would come over to the window, let her dark eyes wander across the deserted cobbles, and then withdraw, without guessing that he was there, filled with anxiety, on the other side of the square. And just as he had trembled at the idea of being seen by her, now he quivered with the need to feel her fix her gaze on him. She was at the forefront of his thoughts every hour of his life.

When Thérèse got up in the morning, he, who had once been so punctual, forgot all about his office. He was still afraid of that white face with its red lips, but his fear gave him an exquisite, sensual thrill. Concealed behind a curtain, he let the terror she filled him with pour through his body, until it made him feel ill, his legs shaking as if he had been walking for hours. He would dream that she suddenly caught sight of him and smiled at him, and that his fear would vanish.

And then he had the idea of seducing her with the help of his flute. On warm evenings, he started to play once more. He left the two casements open, and in the darkness he played his oldest tunes, pastorales as sweet and innocent as little girls dancing in a ring. He played notes that were sustained and tremulous, fading away one after the other in simple cadences, like lovelorn ladies of olden days, twirling their skirts. He would choose moonless nights; the square was pitch black, no one knew where such a sweet melody was coming from as it floated past the sleeping houses on the gentle wings of a nocturnal bird. And, on the very first evening, he was startled to see Thérèse as she prepared for bed coming to the window all in white, and leaning there, surprised to recognise this music she had already heard the day she arrived.

'Just listen, Françoise,' she said in her grave voice, turning to the interior of the room. 'It's not a bird.'

'Oh!' replied an old woman, of whom Julien could make out only the shadow, 'it must be a travelling player having a good time on the outskirts of town – he sounds a long way off.'

'Yes, a long way off,' repeated the girl, after a silence, as she bathed her bare arms in the freshness of the night air.

From then on, every evening, Julien started to play louder. His lips swelled the sound, his feverish desire passed into the old flute of yellow wood. And Thérèse, who listened every evening, was astonished to hear this living music, whose phrases, fluttering from rooftop to rooftop, waited until nightfall before launching on their way towards her. She had the strong impression that the serenade was marching towards her window, she sometimes stood on tiptoes as if to see over the houses. Then, one night, the music broke out so close to her that she felt its breath on her skin; she guessed it was coming from the square, one of those old houses wrapped in sleep. Julien was blowing with the full strength of his passion, the flute was vibrating with crystal chimes. The shadows emboldened him to such an extent that he hoped to bring her to him by the force of his song. And Thérèse did indeed lean forward, as if drawn out and conquered.

'Come back in,' said the voice of the old lady. 'It's a thundery night, you'll have nightmares.'

That night, Julien couldn't sleep. He was sure Thérèse had guessed at his presence, had perhaps even seen him. And he tossed and turned feverishly on his bed, wondering whether or not to show himself the following day. To be sure, it would be ridiculous for him to go on hiding. But he decided that he wouldn't make an appearance, and he was at his window, at six o'clock, putting his flute back in its case, when Thérèse's shutters abruptly opened.

The girl, who never got up before eight, appeared wearing a dressing-gown, and leaned out of the window, her hair twisted on the nape of her neck. Julien remained thunderstruck, staring straight across at her, unable to turn away; meanwhile his hands clumsily and unsuccessfully tried to take his flute apart. Thérèse was examining him, too, with an unblinking, queenly gaze. She seemed for an instant to study his big-boned frame, his huge, rough-hewn body, his whole ugly appearance, that of a timid giant. And she was no longer the feverish child he had seen the night before; she was haughty and very white, with her black eyes and her red lips. When she had made up her mind about him, with the tranquil deliberation she would have brought to deciding whether or not she liked a dog she saw in the street, she passed sentence on him with a light pout; then, turning her back unhurriedly on him, she closed the window.

Julien, his legs turned to jelly, collapsed into his armchair. And broken words emerged from his lips.

'Oh God! She doesn't like me... And I love her, I'm going to die of love!'

He put his head in his hands, he burst into tears. And why on earth had he shown himself? When you are a clodhopper, you hide away, you don't go round frightening the girls. He cursed himself, furious at his ugliness. Shouldn't he have continued to play the flute in the darkness, like a night bird that seduces his listeners' hearts with its song, and must never appear in daylight if it wishes to please? He would have still been for her a sweet music, nothing but the old melody of a mysterious love. She would have adored him without knowing him, like a Prince Charming come from afar to expire with love beneath her window. But, stupid oaf that he was, he had broken the spell. Now she knew he was as thickset as an ox at the plough, and never again would she like his music!

So it turned out: he repeatedly played his tenderest tunes, chose warm nights balmy with the odour of the foliage: it was all in vain, Thérèse wouldn't listen, didn't hear. She came and went in her room, leaned at the window as if he hadn't been right opposite, expressing his love in humble little notes. One day, she even exclaimed: 'Good God, that out-of-tune flute is getting on my nerves!'

Then, in despair, he flung his flute into the back of a drawer and played no more.

It has to be said that young Colombel also made fun of Julien. One day, as he was going to his office, he had seen

Julien at his window, studying one of his pieces, and every time he passed by on the square, he laughed maliciously. Julien knew that the lawyer's clerk received invitations to the Marsanne house, and it broke his heart – not that he was jealous of that little pipsqueak, but because he would have given his right arm to be there for an hour in his place. The young man's mother, Françoise, who had been with the family for years, now looked after Thérèse, whom she had nursed. The noble lady and the little peasant boy had, once upon a time, grown up together, and it seemed natural for them to have kept up something of their old camaraderie. This did not make Julien suffer any the less, however, when he met Colombel in the street, with his pinched, thin-lipped smile. His revulsion grew the day he realised that the little pipsqueak was not bad looking: he had a round head like a cat's, but finely featured, impishly attractive, with green eyes and a sparse beard curling down his snug little chin. Ah! if only he could have got him up against the wall of one of the ramparts, how he would have made him pay dearly for the happiness he enjoyed in seeing Thérèse at her home!

A year went by. Julien was deeply unhappy. He now lived entirely for Thérèse. His heart was imprisoned in that glacial grand house, opposite which he was dying away for clumsiness and love. As soon as he had a free moment, he would spend it there, his eyes fastened to the stretch of grey wall, on which he knew every last patch of moss. He had done all he could, for months on end, to keep his eyes sharp and his ears pricked, he still knew nothing of the inner life of that solemn house into which he projected his whole being. Vague noises, flickers of light left him feeling perplexed. Were they throwing a party, or had someone died? He didn't know, life was on the other side of the house. He would dream as his fancy took him, depending on his moods, grave or gay: Thérèse and Colombel romping noisily, the girl going for a stroll beneath the chestnut trees, balls in which she was twirled in the dancers' arms, sudden occasions of grief that would lead her to sit weeping in dark rooms. Or perhaps all he heard were the light footsteps of the Marquis and Marquise trotting like mice across the old polished floors. And, in his ignorance, he always saw only one window, Thérèse's, piercing that mysterious wall. The girl would appear there, every day, more silent than the stones, but her appearance never gave him the slightest grounds for hope. She threw him into consternation, so unknown and distant did she remain.

Julien's times of greatest happiness came when the window stayed open. Then he could see into the corners of her room, while she was out. It took him six months to discover that the bed was on the left, an alcove bed, with pink silk curtains. Then, after another six months, he realised that opposite the bed was a Louis-Quinze chest of drawers topped by a mirror in a china frame. Opposite that, he could make out the white marble fireplace. This bedroom was the paradise he dreamt of.

His love did not spare him immense struggles. He would hide away for weeks, ashamed at his ugliness. Then he would be filled with rage. He needed to stretch his bulky limbs, to impose on her the sight of his pitted face burning with fever. Then he would spend weeks at the window, wearing her out with the sight of him. Twice, he even blew her ardent kisses, with all the brutality of shy people when they are driven mad by daring.

Thérèse didn't even lose her temper. When he was hidden, he could see her coming and going with her royal demeanour, and when he forced her to see him, she maintained the same attitude, only even more haughty and frigid. He never caught her losing her self-control. If her eyes happened to encounter him, she made no haste to look away. When he heard people in the post office say that Mlle de Marsanne was deeply pious and charitable, he would sometimes protest violently to himself. No, no! she was completely irreligious, she loved blood for she had blood on her lips, and the pallor of her face came from her contempt for the world. Then he would weep for having insulted her, and beg her for forgiveness, as if she were a saint enfolded in the purity of her wings.

Throughout this first year, day followed on after day without bringing any change. When summer returned, he experienced a peculiar sensation: Thérèse seemed to him to be walking in another atmosphere. There were the same little events as before, the shutters were pushed open each morning and closed again in the evening, there were the regular appearances at the usual hours; but a new spirit emanated from her room. Thérèse was paler, taller. One feverish day he took the risk of blowing her a third kiss from his fevered fingertips. She looked at him fixedly, her gravity disconcerting, without leaving the window. He was the one to withdraw, his face flushed.

There was only one new development, towards the end of the summer – one that shook him to the depths of his being, even though it was the simplest little thing imaginable. Almost every day, at dusk, Thérèse's casement, which had been left half-open, would be violently slammed shut, making the wooden panels and the window catch clatter. This bang would make Julien jump in painful trepidation; and he was left tormented with anxiety, his heart bruised, without being able to say why. After this abrupt detonation, the house relapsed into such a deathly quiet that the silence made him afraid. For a long time, he was unable to make out whose arm it was slamming the window shut like that; but, one evening, he caught sight of Thérèse's pale hands; she it was twisting the window catch to with such impatient fury. And when, an hour later, she reopened the window, but slowly this time, with a dignified deliberation, she seemed weary, leaning for a moment on the window sill; then she would walk up and down in her immaculate room, attending to girlish little occupations. Julien was left standing vacantly, and the continual scrape of the window catch echoed in his ears.

One grey, mild autumn evening, the catch gave a terrible squeal. Julien shuddered, and involuntary tears fell from his eyes, as he looked over at the gloomy house immersed in the shadows of twilight. It had rained that morning, the half-bare chestnut trees were giving off an odour of death.

But Julien continued to wait for the window to reopen. And suddenly it did reopen, just as violently as it had closed. Thérèse appeared. She was completely white, her eyes wide open, her hair hanging loose round her neck. She stood there at the window, she put her ten fingers to her red lips, and blew Julien a kiss.

Distraught, he pressed his fists to his chest, as if to ask whether this kiss was meant for him.

Then Thérèse thought he was withdrawing. She leaned out further, again set her ten fingers to her red lips, and blew him a second kiss, and then a third. It was as if she were returning the young man's three kisses. He stood there gaping. It was a clear evening, he could see her distinctly outlined in the window's shadowy frame.

When she thought she had won him, she glanced down into the small square. And, in a strained voice: 'Come,' she said simply.

He came. He went downstairs, walked over to the house. As he was looking up, the front door half opened, that door which had been locked and bolted for perhaps half a century, and whose hinged leaves had been bound together by moss. But he walked along in a stupor, no longer surprised at anything. The moment he went in, the door closed behind him, and he was led along by a small icy hand. He went upstairs, along a corridor, across a first room, and finally found himself in a bedroom that he recognised. It was paradise, the room with the pink silk curtains. The daylight was dwindling away slowly and gently. He was tempted to fall to his knees. But Thérèse was standing bolt upright in front of him, her hands tightly clasped, so full of resolve that she managed to repress the shudders that were running up and down her.

'Do you love me?' she asked in a low voice.

'Oh yes! Oh yes!' he stammered.

But she signalled him not to waste his breath on useless babble. She resumed, in a haughty tone that seemed to make her words natural and chaste as they came from her girlish lips: 'If I gave myself to you, you'd do anything, wouldn't you?'

Unable to reply, he folded his hands together. For a kiss from her, he would sell his soul.

'Well, I've got a favour to ask you.'

As he remained dumb, she broke out into sudden violence, feeling utterly exhausted and sensing that she might soon run out of courage. She cried, 'Look, we've got to swear to it first... I swear to keep my side of the bargain... Go on, you swear too!'

'Oh, I swear! Oh, whatever you want!' he said, in a moment of total self-abandonment.

The pure clean smell of the room made his senses swim.

The curtains round the alcove were drawn to, and the mere thought of her virginal bed, in the soft shadow of pink silk, threw him into a religious ecstasy. Then, with her suddenly brutal hands, she tore apart the curtains and revealed the alcove, into which the twilight shed a sinister gleam. The bed was in disorder, the sheets trailing down, a pillow that had fallen to the ground seemed dented by tooth marks. And, in the midst of the crumpled lace, lay the body of a man, barefoot, sprawling sideways.

'There,' she explained in a choked voice, 'that man was my lover… I pushed him, he fell over, I just don't know. Anyway, he's dead… And you've got to take him away. Do you understand?… That's all, yes, that's all. That's what you must do!'

3

While still a little girl, Thérèse de Marsanne took Colombel for her stooge. He was barely six months older than she was, and Françoise, his mother, had ended up bottle-feeding him, so as to give her own milk to Thérèse. Later on, having grown up in the household, he took on a vague position somewhere between servant boy and playmate for the little girl.

Thérèse was an *enfant terrible*. It wasn't that she was a noisy tomboy. She maintained, on the contrary, a singular gravity, which led to her being considered a well brought-up young lady by the visitors to whom she would curtsey so charmingly. But she had strange whims: she would suddenly burst out into inarticulate cries, and stamp her feet in a wild tantrum when she was alone; or she would lie on her back in the middle of one of the garden paths, and stay there, stretched out, obstinately refusing to get up, despite the punishments they sometimes decided to mete out to her.

No one could ever tell what she was thinking. Already, in

those big childish eyes of hers, she extinguished every spark of life; and, in place of those clear mirrors where the souls of little girls can be seen so clearly, she had two dark holes, deep and black as ink, in which it was impossible to read.

At the age of six, she started to torture Colombel. He was small and puny. So she would lead him to the bottom of the garden, under the chestnut trees, to a place well hidden by the shade of the leaves, and leap on his back, forcing him to carry her. She straddled him for hour-long rides round a wide clump in the middle. She clasped him round the neck, digging her heels repeatedly into his ribs, giving him no chance to draw breath. He was the horse, she the fine lady. When, overcome by dizziness, he seemed on the point of collapse, she would bite his ear until she drew blood, squeezing him so fiercely that her small fingernails pierced his flesh. And on they galloped, this cruel six-year-old queen riding through the trees, her hair streaming in the wind, on the back of the boy she was using as her steed.

Later, when they were with her parents, she would pinch him, and forbid him to cry out, under the permanent threat of having him thrown out onto the streets if he said anything about their little games. In this way they led a sort of secret life, a shared existence, which changed when they were in company. When they were alone, she treated him as a toy, often feeling the urge to break him open, curious to find out what was inside. Was she not a marquise, did she not see people at her feet the whole time? Since she had been given a little man to play with, she was at perfect liberty to do with him what her fancy dictated. And when she got bored of tyrannising Colombel far from people's eyes, she would give herself the added and even more intense pleasure of dealing him a hefty kick or sticking a pin in his arm in the midst of a big group of visitors, while hypnotising him with her dark eyes so he would not so much as flinch.

Colombel put up with this martyr's life, despite moments of mute revolt which left him trembling, his eyes downcast, struggling to overcome the temptation of strangling his young mistress. But he himself was sly by temperament. He had no great objection to being beaten. He derived a sour enjoyment from it, and sometimes arranged things so he would get pricked, waiting for the needle to enter his flesh with a shudder of fierce satisfaction; and then he would become absorbed in the delightful prospect of getting his own back. In any case, he was already taking his revenge, deliberately falling onto hard stones and dragging Thérèse down with him, unafraid of breaking a limb, and all too pleased when she picked up bumps and grazes. If he didn't cry out when she pinched him in company, it was so no one would intervene between them. It was their business, that was all, a quarrel from which he intended to emerge the victor later on.

Meanwhile, however, the Marquis was worried by his daughter's violent manners. People said that she resembled one of her uncles, who had led a life fraught with terrible adventures, and who had died murdered in a den of vice in some out-of-the-way suburb. Indeed, a seam of tragedy ran through the whole history of the Marsanne family; every so often, their members were born with a strange malady, despite their dignified and haughty lineage; and this malady was like an outbreak of madness, a perverse emotional disorder, an upwelling of scum which seemed for a while to rid the family of the impurity. So the Marquis thought it wise to submit Thérèse to a strict education, and he placed her in a convent, where he hoped the discipline would make her more tractable. She stayed there until she was eighteen.

When Thérèse came home, she was very well behaved and very tall. Her parents were happy to see that she had developed a profound sense of piety. In church, she would remain deep in prayer, her forehead in her hands. At home, she spread about her an odour of innocence and peace. Only one small failing could be held against her: she was greedy; she ate sweets from morning to evening, sucking them with half-closed eyes, her red lips quivering slightly. No one would have recognised the mute and obstinate child who often returned from the garden with her clothes in shreds, refusing to say what games she had been playing to get all torn like that. The Marquis and Marquise, who had lived secluded for fifteen years in the depths of their empty residence, thought it was time to reopen their salon. They laid on a few dinner parties for the local nobility. They even held dances. Their plan was to marry Thérèse off. And, for all her coldness, she went along, dressing up and waltzing, but with such a white face that she unsettled the young men who ventured to fall in love with her.

Never had Thérèse said anything further about young Colombel. The Marquis had made arrangements for him and had just found him a position with M. Savournin the lawyer, after ensuring he had received a basic education. One day, Françoise, having brought her son along, thrust him forward in front of Thérèse, reminding the girl that he had once been her playmate. Colombel was smiling, spotlessly clean, quite unaffected. Thérèse looked at him calmly, said that, yes indeed, she did remember, then turned away. But a week later, Colombel returned, and soon he had resumed his former habits. He came to the house every evening, after work at the lawyer's, bringing pieces of music, books, and albums. He was treated as if of no importance, and given errands to do, like a servant or a poor relative. He was a dependent of the family. So no one thought it amiss to leave him alone with the girl. Just as they had done long ago, they closeted themselves together in the big rooms, they spent hours under the leaves of the garden trees. Truth to tell, they no longer played the same games there. Thérèse walked slowly along, her dress swooshing gently through the grass. Colombel, dressed like the rich young men of the town, accompanied her, prodding the earth with a supple cane he always carried with him.

However, she slowly turned back into the queen and he into her slave. To be sure, she no longer bit him, but she had a way of walking next to him which, little by little, made him feel even smaller, changed him into a court lackey, holding up his sovereign lady's robe. She tormented him with her whimsical moods, pouring out words of affection, and then becoming harsh, simply to entertain herself. He, on the other hand, would wait for her to look away and then dart a bright-eyed glance at her, as piercing as a sword thrust, and his whole body would stretch out its depraved young limbs as he watched and waited for the moment to enact the dreamt-of betrayal.

One summer evening, under the heavy foliage of the chestnut trees, they had been walking for quite a while when Thérèse, after a period of silence, asked him gravely, 'I say, Colombel, I'm really tired. What if you carried me, remember, like you used to?'

He laughed a little. Then, perfectly seriously, he answered, 'My pleasure, Thérèse.'

But she resumed her walk, saying simply, 'It's all right, I just wanted to know.'

They carried on walking. Night was falling, there was deep shadow beneath the trees. They talked about a lady in town who had just married an officer. As they were entering a narrower path, the young man moved to step aside and let her pass first; but she pushed against him violently, forcing him to walk ahead. Now they were both silent.

And, all at once, Thérèse leapt onto Colombel's spine, with all the suppleness she had once had as a fierce little girl.

'Right, off you go!' she said, her voice changed, choked with the passion of former times.

She had torn the cane from his hands, and was beating his thighs with it. Clasping his shoulders, squeezing him tight enough to suffocate him between her vigorous horsewoman's legs, she rode him wildly on through the dark shadowy undergrowth. She whipped him long and hard, spurring him on faster and faster. Colombel's headlong gallop had him panting for breath over the grass. He hadn't uttered a single word, he was breathing hard, stiffening on his stocky little legs, feeling this big girl's warm weight crushing his neck.

But, when she shouted, 'Enough!', he didn't stop. He galloped even faster, as if carried away by his own momentum. His hands, clasped behind him, were holding her so tightly round the knees that she couldn't jump off. Now it was the horse that was filled with fury and carrying off its mistress. All at once, in spite of the stinging lashes of the cane and the scratches, he sped towards a shed that the gardener kept his tools in. There, he threw her to the ground, and he raped her on the straw. Finally, his turn had come to be the master.

Thérèse grew even paler, her lips redder and her eyes darker. She carried on with her life of piety. Some days later, the same scene happened all over again: she leapt onto Colombel's back, tried to tame him, and again ended by being flung onto the straw of the shed. When they were in company, she treated him gently, continuing to show him the condescending attitude of a big sister. He too put on a demeanour of smiling serenity. They remained, as at the age of six, wild beasts, let loose and secretly amusing themselves with their bites. Now, however, the male was victorious when the hour struck for the disorders of desire.

Their love-life was tempestuous. Thérèse received Colombel in her bedroom. She had let him have a key to the little garden door, which opened onto the narrow street on the ramparts. At night, he was obliged to cross a first room in which slept his mother, of all people. But the lovers deployed such tranquil self-assurance that they were never surprised together. They went so far as to arrange to meet in broad daylight. Colombel arrived before dinner, Thérèse would be waiting for him, and the window closed so the neighbours wouldn't see. At every hour of the day they felt the need to see each other, not to exchange the endearments of twenty-year-old lovers, but to resume the battle of their pride. Often, a quarrel would shake them, they traded insults in low tones, trembling with an anger all the more intense as they could not yield to their longing to shout out and fight.

So it was that one evening, before dinner, Colombel had come. Then, as he was pacing up and down in the bedroom, still barefoot and in shirtsleeves, he had had the idea of grabbing Thérèse and lifting her in the way a fairground strong man might when limbering up for a bout of wrestling. Thérèse tried to struggle free, saying, 'Leave me alone, you know I'm stronger than you. I'd hurt you.'

Colombel laughed softly.

'All right! Go on, hurt me,' he murmured.

He was still shaking her, trying to bring her down. Then she folded her arms. They often played this game, yearning to do battle. As often as not, it was Colombel who fell flat on his back on the carpet, suffocating, his limbs floppy and slack. He was too small, she would pull him up and squeeze him against her with the grip of a giantess.

But, on this particular day, Thérèse slipped to her knees, and Colombel, suddenly lashing out, knocked her over. He stood there, exulting.

'See, you're not the strongest,' he said with a derisory laugh.

She had turned pale with fury. She slowly got up, and, speechless, flew at him again, shaking with such anger that he in turn shuddered. Oh! if only she could strangle him, be rid of him, have him there inert, vanquished once and for all! For a minute they wrestled without a word, panting for breath, their bones cracking in their grip. And now it was no longer a game. The cold wind of murder was beating about their heads. He started to choke. She, afraid that they might be heard, pushed him over with one last terrible effort. His temple struck the corner of the chest of drawers, he fell heavily and lay full length on the ground.

Thérèse spent a minute getting her breath back. She tidied her hair in the mirror, smoothed out her skirt, affecting not to pay any attention to the defeated man. He could pick himself up. Then, she poked him with her foot. And, as he remained motionless, she finally bent over him, a chill running through the stray locks of hair at the back of her neck. Then, she saw Colombel's face, white and waxen, his eyes glazed, his mouth twisted. On his right temple, there was a hole; the temple had been smashed in as he fell against the corner of the chest of drawers. Colombel was dead.

She straightened up, numb. She spoke out loud, into the silence.

'Dead! Just look at him now, dead!'

And, all at once, the reality of the situation filled her with a dreadful anguish. Doubtless she had indeed, for a second, wanted to kill him. But this thought, inspired by anger, was silly. You always want to kill people when you're fighting; but you never do kill them, because dead people are too much of a nuisance. No, no, she wasn't guilty, she'd never wanted that. In her own bedroom, just imagine!

She continued to talk to herself, the broken words tumbling from her lips: 'Well it's all over... He's dead, he won't get out of here by himself.'

The cold stupor of the first moments was succeeded in her by a fever rising from her belly to her throat, like a wave of fire. She had a dead man in her bedroom. She would never be able to explain what he was doing there, barefoot, in shirtsleeves, with a hole in his temple. Her situation was hopeless.

Thérèse leant down to examine the wound. But terror froze her as she stood over the corpse. She heard Françoise, Colombel's mother, going along the corridor. Other noises were audible, footsteps, voices, preparations for a party which was due to happen that same day. They might call her, come looking for her from one moment to the next. And that dead man lying there, the lover she had killed who was now a weight on her shoulders, crushing her with the burden of their illicit relationship!

Then, deafened by the clamour growing ever louder in her skull, she straightened up and began to pace round and round in her room. She was looking for a hole in which to throw this body that now obstructed her future, she looked under all the furniture, in every corner, shaking from head to foot, trembling with rage at her powerlessness. No, there wasn't a hole, the alcove was not deep enough, the wardrobes were not wide enough, the whole bedroom refused to offer her any help. And yet it was there that they had exchanged their kisses in secret! He had come softly padding in like a sly tom-cat and had then padded off again. Never could she have believed he would be such a burden.

Thérèse was still capering with impatience, loping round the room with the crazy dance of a hunted beast, when she suddenly seemed to have an inspired idea. What if she threw Colombel out of the window? But he would be found, it would be easy to guess where he had fallen from. However, she had already lifted the curtain to look out onto the street; and, all at once, she noticed the young man in the house opposite, that flute-playing fool leaning out of his window with his usual hangdog appearance. She knew all too well his pale face, always turned to gaze at her, and which she had wearied of, as she could read such despicable tenderness in it. The sight of Julien, so humble and so loving, brought her up short. A smile lit up her pale face. That was where her safety lay. The fool opposite loved her with the devotion of a chained mastiff, which would obediently follow her into crime. Furthermore, she would compensate him with all her heart, with all her flesh. She had not loved him, as he was too gentle; but love him she would, she would buy him forever with the faithful gift of her body, if he dipped his hands in blood for her. Her red lips quivered momentarily, as at the taste of a terror-stricken love whose novelty allured her.

Then, with sudden energy, as if she had been picking up a bundle of linen, she lifted Colombel's body and dragged it onto the bed. And, opening the window, she blew kisses to Julien.

4

Julien was pacing around in a nightmare. When he recognised Colombel on the bed, he was not surprised, he found it natural and simple. Yes, it could only be Colombel in the recesses of that alcove, his temple smashed in, his limbs sprawled out, in a pose of dreadful lust.

But meanwhile, Thérèse was talking to him at length. At first he did not hear, the words poured into his stupefied mind with a noise of confusion. Then, he realised that she was giving him orders, and he listened. He must not leave the bedroom now, but stay there until midnight, waiting for the house to be dark and empty. This party that the Marquis was giving would prevent them from acting any earlier; but in the final analysis it presented them with favourable circumstances, preoccupying everyone too much for them to think of coming upstairs to look for the girl. When the time came, Julien would lift the corpse onto his back, go down and throw it into the Chanteclair, at the bottom of the rue Beau-Soleil. Nothing could be easier, to judge from the tranquillity with which Thérèse explained the whole plan.

She stopped, and then, laying her hands on the young man's shoulders, she asked, 'You've understood then, it's all agreed?'

He gave a start.

'Yes, yes, anything you want. I am all yours.'

Then, gravely, she leant forward. As he didn't understand what she wanted, she continued, 'Kiss me.'

He planted a kiss on her icy forehead, shuddering. And both remained silent.

Thérèse had drawn shut the curtains round the bed. She sank into an armchair, where at last she rested, engulfed in the shadows. Julien, after remaining on his feet for a few minutes, also sat down on a chair. Françoise had left the room next door, only muffled noises came from the house, the room seemed to be sleeping as it slowly filled with darkness.

For almost an hour, nothing moved. Julien could hear,

beating against his skull, heavy throbs that stopped him following any rational train of thought. He was in Thérèse's room, and this filled him with happiness. Then, all at once, when he came to reflect that a man's corpse was also there, in the recesses of that alcove whose curtains, as they grazed his skin, made him shudder, he felt faint. She had loved that little pipsqueak, good God! was it possible? He could forgive her for having killed him; what fired his blood was the sight of Colombel's bare feet lying amidst the lacy bedclothes. How glad he would be to throw him into the Chanteclair, off the end of the bridge, into a deep dark spot that he knew well! They would both be rid of him, they would be able to have each other afterwards. Then, at the thought of that bliss he had not dared to dream of only that morning, he abruptly saw himself on the bed, on the very place where the corpse now lay, and the place was cold, and he felt a terrified revulsion.

Leaning far back into the depths of the armchair, Thérèse was motionless. Against the indistinct light of the window, he could just make out the high outline of her chignon. She sat with her face in her hands, and it was not possible to know the feelings that were thus overwhelming her. Was it a mere physical reaction to the terrible crisis she had just been through? Was it stifled remorse, was she sorry for that lover now sleeping his last sleep? Was she calmly hatching her escape plan, or was she concealing the ravages of fear on her face immersed in shadow? He could not guess.

The clock chimed, breaking the deep silence. Then, Thérèse rose slowly to her feet, lit the candles on her dressing-table; and she appeared in all her customary calm composure, rested and strong. She seemed to have forgotten the body lolling behind the pink silk curtains as she walked up and down in her room at the unhurried pace of a person with things to do in the sequestered tranquillity of her own room. Then, as she was letting down her hair, she said without even turning round, 'I'm going to get dressed for this party… If anyone were to come, you could hide at the back of the alcove, all right?'

He continued to sit in his chair, looking at her. She was already treating him as a lover, as if the bloody complicity she had created between them had had the effect of a long liaison, allowing them to know each other intimately.

Her arms lifted, she dressed her hair. He was still gazing at her with a tremor, so desirable was she, with her bare back, delicate elbows casually flexing, and slender hands busy curling her hair. So was she trying to seduce him, to show him the mistress he was going to win, and thereby inspire him with courage?

She had just put on her shoes, when they heard footsteps.

'Hide in the alcove,' she said in a low voice.

And, with a deft movement, she threw over Colombel's stiff body all the underclothes she had just taken off, clothes still warm and imbued with her perfume.

It was Françoise who came in, saying, 'They are waiting for you, mademoiselle.'

'I'm coming, my dear,' Thérèse tranquilly replied. 'Just a minute! You can help me put on my dress.'

Julien, through a narrow gap in the curtains, could see the two women, and he shuddered at the girl's boldness, his teeth chattering so loudly that he had gripped his jaw hard to stop anyone hearing. Right next to him, beneath the woman's undershirt, he could see one of Colombel's icy feet dangling. Imagine if Françoise, Colombel's mother, had drawn the curtain aside and happened across her son's foot, that bare foot sticking out!

34

'Be careful,' Thérèse was repeating, 'slow down: you're pulling the flowers off.'

Her voice was expressionless. She was smiling now, like any girl glad to be going to the ball. The dress was a white silk dress, covered all over with wild roses, their flowers white with a red-hued tip at their heart. And, when she stood in the middle of the room, she was like a great bouquet, virginal in her whiteness. Her bare arms, her bare neck blended into the whiteness of the silk.

'Oh! how beautiful you look, how beautiful you look!' old Françoise kept repeating with satisfaction. 'And wait, don't forget your garland!'

She seemed to be searching for it, and reached out to the curtains, as if to have a look on the bed. Julien almost let out a cry of anguish. But Thérèse, quite unhurried, still smiling at herself in the mirror, continued: 'My garland is over there, look, on the chest of drawers. Give it to me... Oh! don't touch my bed. I've put my things there. You'd mess it all up.'

Françoise helped her to put on the long rose branch she wore as a crown, the end of which curled down onto her neck. Then, Thérèse stood there for one minute longer, admiring her appearance. She was ready, just slipping on her gloves.

'Ah yes!' Françoise exclaimed, 'there isn't a single young girl as pure and white as you, in church!'

This compliment again made the girl smile. She gazed at herself one last time and headed to the door, saying, 'Come on, let's go down... You can blow out the candles.'

In the sudden darkness that fell, Julien heard the door closing shut and Thérèse's dress moving away, its silk rustling along the corridor. He sat on the floor, in the corner between bed and wall, not yet daring to leave the alcove. The deep night veiled his sight; but he could still feel, right near him, the sensation of that bare foot, which seemed to spread a chill through the whole room. He had been there he didn't know for how long, weighed down by a heavy, almost soporific mass of thoughts, when the door was opened again. From the swoosh of the silk, he recognised Thérèse. She didn't move forward, but simply placed something on the chest of drawers, murmuring, 'Here, you must have gone without your dinner… You've got to eat, all right?'

The faint rustle of the silk was heard again, the dress moved away a second time, down the corridor. Julien, shaken, rose to his feet. He was suffocating in the alcove, he couldn't stay sitting against that bed any longer, next to Colombel. The clock struck eight, he had four hours to wait. Then, he walked forward, muffling the sound of his footsteps.

A feeble glimmer, coming from the starry night, enabled him to distinguish the dark shapes of the furniture. Some of the corners were immersed in darkness. Alone, the mirror preserved a dull reflection of old silver. He was not usually prone to fear; but, in this room, trickles of sweat at times drenched his face. Around him, dark looming furniture shifted, assuming menacing shapes. Three times he thought he heard sighs emerging from the alcove. And each time he froze, terrified. Then, when he listened more closely, they turned out to be noises rising up from the party, a dance tune, the murmurous laughter of a crowd. He closed his eyes; and, suddenly, instead of the black hole of the bedroom, there would be an abrupt dazzling light, a brilliantly lit salon, in which he could see Thérèse, with her pure dress, swinging past to an amorous rhythm, in the arms of a waltzer. The whole house was throbbing to the strains of joyful music. He was alone, in this abominable hole, shivering with dread. At one moment, he recoiled, his hair standing on end: he thought he could see a light starting to glow on a seat. When he plucked up the courage to go and touch it, he recognised a white satin corset. He took it, buried his face in the fabric that had been softly moulded by the young horsewoman's slender breast, slowly breathing in its odour, to numb his senses.

Ah! what rapture! He wanted to forget everything. No, this was no vigil for the dead, it was a vigil of love. He went over to the window and pressed his forehead to the pane, still holding the satin corset to his lips; and he started to go over the story of his passion. Opposite, on the other side of the street, he could make out his room, whose windows had stayed open. It was there that he had seduced Thérèse in his long evenings of fervent music. His flute would sing with tenderness, pour out his declarations, with such a sweet tremulousness in its timid lover's voice that the girl, vanquished, had finally smiled. This satin he was kissing was her satin, a corner of the satin of her skin, which she had left for him so he would not lose patience. His dream started to become so vivid that he left the window and ran over to the door, thinking he could hear her.

The chill atmosphere of the room fell on his shoulders; and, coming down to earth, he remembered. Then, he was seized by a furious resolve. Ah! he would hesitate no longer, he would come back that same night. She was too beautiful, he was too much in love with her. When two people's love is sealed by crime, their love must be passionate enough to make their bones crack. To be sure, he would return, he would come running back without wasting a moment, as soon as the bundle had been dumped in the river. And, driven wild, shaken by a nervous spasm, he sank his teeth into the satin corset, rolling his head in the fabric, trying to stifle his sobs of desire.

Ten o'clock struck. He listened. He felt he had been there

for years. So he waited, in a complete daze. His hand brushed against some bread and fruit, and he ate standing, hungrily, with an ache in his stomach that he could not soothe. This food would give him strength, perhaps. Then, when he had eaten, he was overwhelmed by an immense weariness. The night seemed as if it would drag on forever. In the house, the distant music became more distinct; at times the thump of a dance shook the polished floor; carriages were starting to roll away. And as he gazed fixedly at the door, he saw what looked like a star shining through the keyhole. He didn't even bother to hide. Too bad if someone came in!

'No thanks, Françoise,' said Thérèse, appearing with a candle. 'I can get undressed by myself... You go to bed, you must be tired.'

She pushed the door to, and slid the bolt across. Then, she stood motionless for a moment, a finger at her lips, still holding the candlestick. The dance had brought no flush to her cheeks. She said nothing, set down the candlestick, sat opposite Julien. For another half an hour, they waited, gazing at each other.

The doors had slammed shut, the house was drifting off to sleep. But what worried Thérèse more than anything was the proximity of Françoise, that bedroom in which the old woman lived. Françoise walked up and down for a few minutes, then her bed creaked, she had just lain down on it. For a long time she twisted and turned in her sheets, as if unable to get to sleep. Finally the sound of strong regular breathing could be heard through the dividing wall.

Thérèse was still gazing at Julien, gravely. She uttered just two words.

'Come on,' she said.

They drew the curtains, and set about dressing young

Colombel's corpse, which had already started to stiffen into a lugubrious puppet. When this task was completed, both their foreheads were drenched with sweat.

'Come on!' she said a second time.

Julien, without hesitating, in one single movement grasped young Colombel and swung him across his shoulders, in the same way that butchers carry calves. His big frame sagged under the weight, the corpse's feet dangled a yard above the ground.

'I'll walk ahead of you,' murmured Thérèse rapidly. 'I'll hold you by your jacket, you'll just need to let me guide you. And go slowly.'

They first had to get through Françoise's room. This was the most daunting part. They had crossed the room when one of the corpse's feet bumped against a chair. At the noise, Françoise awoke. They heard her raise her head, muttering and mumbling. And they froze – she glued to the door, he crushed under the weight of the body, overcome by fear that the mother would catch them carting her son off to the river. For a minute they endured the most atrocious anguish. Then, Françoise appeared to go back to sleep, and they made their way out into the corridor, cautiously.

But there, they were thrown into panic again. The Marquise had not yet gone to bed, a streak of light was gleaming through her half-opened door. At that moment they dared go neither forward nor backward. Julien felt as if young Colombel would slip off his shoulders if he were forced to cross Françoise's room a second time. For almost a quarter of an hour, they did not move; and Thérèse had the dreadful courage to help support the corpse so Julien would not exhaust himself. Finally the streak of light went out, they were able to reach the ground floor. They were saved.

It was Thérèse who forced half-open once more the old blocked-up carriage entrance. And, when Julien found himself in the middle of the Place des Quatre-Femmes, his burden on his back, he saw her standing there, at the top of the steps, her arms bare, all white in her ball gown. She would be waiting for him.

5

Julien had the strength of a bull. As a child, in the forest near his village, he had enjoyed helping the woodcutters, loading tree trunks onto his boyish shoulders. So he could carry young Colombel as if he were as light as a feather. That pip-squeak's corpse was like a bird round his neck. He hardly felt him, he was seized with a malevolent joy at finding how little he weighed, how slender he was, how completely insub-stantial. Never again would young Colombel snigger as he passed beneath his window, on the days he played the flute; he would no longer pepper him with his jokes in town. And, at the thought that he had in his grasp a successful rival now stiff and cold, Julien felt his loins quiver with satisfaction. He hiked him up round his neck, gritted his teeth and stepped out.

The town was dark. But there was light on the Place des Quatre-Femmes, at the window of Captain Pidoux; probably the captain was unwell, the swollen outline of his belly could be seen coming and going behind the curtains. Julien, in trepidation, was slipping past the houses opposite when the sound of a slight cough froze him. He halted in the shadow of a doorway, recognising the wife of the lawyer Savournin, taking the air and looking up at the skies as she heaved heavy sighs. It was sheer bad luck; usually, at this hour, the Place des Quatre-Femmes was fast asleep. Mme Savournin, fortunately, finally went back home to lay her head on the pillow next to M. Savournin, whose rumbling snores could be heard in the cobbled street, floating down through the window. And, when this window was at last closed, Julien swiftly crossed the square, still keeping an eye open for the twisted, dancing silhouette of Captain Pidoux.

Nonetheless, he felt reassured once he had reached the constricted thoroughfare of the rue Beau-Soleil. There, the houses were so close together, the cobbled street twisted down so steeply, that the starlight could not penetrate to the bottom of this narrow lane, in which a pool of dense shadow seemed to have gathered. As soon as he saw how sheltered he was, an irresistible desire to run impelled him suddenly into a furious gallop. It was dangerous and stupid, he was perfectly aware of that; but he couldn't stop himself galloping, he could still sense at his back the clear empty square of the Place des Quatre-Femmes, with the windows of the lawyer's wife and the captain lit up like two big eyes gazing at him. His shoes made such a racket on the cobbles that he thought he was being pursued. Then, all at once, he stopped. Thirty yards away, he had just heard the voices of the officers staying at the guest-house run by a blonde widow in the rue Beau-Soleil. These gentlemen must have decided to indulge in a bowl of punch to celebrate the transfer of one of their comrades. The young man told himself that, if they came back up the street, he would have had it; there was no side-street down which he could escape, and he would certainly not have time to turn back. He listened to the regular tread of their boots and the light clatter of their swords, and was overwhelmed with a suffocating panic. For a few moments, he was unable to work out whether the sounds were approaching or receding. But the noises slowly faded away. He waited a little longer, then decided to continue his journey, muffling the sound of his footsteps. He would have gone barefoot if he had dared pause long enough to take off his shoes.

Finally, Julien emerged in front of the town gate.

There is no toll-house there, nor any kind of guard post. So he could pass freely. But the sudden expanse of countryside opening up before him terrified him, as he came out of the narrow rue Beau-Soleil. The countryside was blue all over, a soft gentle blue colour; a fresh breeze was blowing; and it seemed to him that a huge crowd was waiting for him there, breathing into his face. They could see him, there would be a terrible outcry that would root him to the spot.

But the bridge lay before him. He could see the white road, the two parapets, low and grey like benches of granite; he could hear the murmur of the Chanteclair making crystal-clear music in the tall weeds. Then he ventured forward, walking bent double, avoiding the open spaces, afraid of being seen by the thousand mute witnesses he sensed all around him. The most alarming part was the bridge itself, on which he would be exposed to the view of the whole town, built like an amphitheatre all around. And he wanted to get to the end of the bridge, to the place where he habitually sat, his legs dangling, breathing in the fresh air of fine evenings. Where the bed of the Chanteclair formed a deep hollow, there was a still, black stretch of water, dimpled by fleeting wrinkles from the hidden turbulence of a violent whirlpool. How many times had he amused himself by throwing stones into this stretch of water so as to measure by the bubbling of the water the depth of the river at that point! He made one last effort of will-power, and crossed the bridge.

Yes, this was the place. Julien recognised the slab, worn smooth by his long sojourns there. He bent over, he could see the stretch of water with its swift dimples, tracing smiles. This was the place, and he unloaded his burden onto the parapet. Before throwing young Colombel in, he felt an irresistible urge to look at him one last time. The eyes of all the townspeople gazing at him would have been unable to prevent him satisfying his wish. He stood for a few seconds face to face with the corpse. The hole in its temple had blackened. A cart, in the distance of the sleeping countryside, was making a great moaning noise. Then Julien made haste; and to avoid too noisy a splash, he hauled the body over and helped it down. But, he couldn't tell how, the dead man's arms clasped him round his neck so powerfully that he himself was dragged down. Miraculously, he managed to grab hold of a ridge. Young Colombel had wanted to take him with him.

When he came to himself, sitting on the slab, he felt faint. He remained there, worn-out, his back bent, his legs dangling, in the same slack-limbed posture of a weary rambler that he had so often fallen into. And he stared down at the still stretch of water, where the merry dimples were starting to reappear. There was no doubt about it, young Colombel had wanted to take him with him; he had grabbed him by the neck, dead though he was. But none of these things existed any more; he breathed deeply the fresh countryside smell; his eyes followed the silvery reflection on the river between the velvety shadows of the trees; and this corner of nature seemed to be a promise of peace, of endless cradling, in a discreet and secret bliss.

Then, he remembered Thérèse. She would be waiting for him, he was sure. He could see her still at the top of the ruined steps, on the threshold of the door with its moss-covered wood. She was standing erect, in her white satin dress, adorned with wild roses, with a red-hued tip at their heart. But perhaps she had started to feel the cold. Then, she must have gone up to wait for him in her room. She had left the door open, she had lain down on the bed, like a bride on the evening of her wedding day.

Ah! what a sweet prospect! Never before had a woman waited for him like that. A minute later, he would be at the promised assignation. But his legs were growing numb, he was afraid he might fall asleep. Was he a coward then? And, to rouse himself, he imagined Thérèse at her dressing-table, when she had let her clothes fall. He saw her with her arms lifted, her bosom stretched, her delicate elbows and pale hands flexing. He whipped up his ardour with his memories, thinking of the fragrance she exuded, her supple skin, that bedroom of terrible pleasures in which he had drunk in such intoxicating madness. Was he going to renounce all that offered passion, the foretaste of which was burning his lips? No, he would rather drag himself there on his knees, if his legs refused to carry him.

But this was a battle he had already lost, in which his vanquished love was in its final death throes. He had only one irresistible need – to sleep, to sleep forever. The image of Thérèse was growing fainter, a great black wall was rising up to separate them. Now he wouldn't have been able to touch her shoulder lightly with his fingertip without dying. As his desire expired, it gave off the smell of a corpse. It was all becoming impossible, the ceiling would have fallen in on their heads if he had returned to the bedroom and pressed that girl to his flesh.

To sleep, to sleep forever, how nice that must be, when you no longer had anything in you worth the pleasure of staying awake for! He wouldn't go to the post office the next day, it was no use; he wouldn't play the flute again, he wouldn't sit at his window. So, why not sleep for good? His life was over, it was time for bed. And he again looked at the river, trying to see

44

if young Colombel was still there. Colombel was an intelligent lad: he knew for sure what he was doing, when he had tried to take Julien with him.

The stretch of water spread out, dotted by the fleeting laughter of its whirlpools. The Chanteclair murmured as sweetly as music, while the countryside opened up shadowy expanses of supreme peace. Julien stammered Thérèse's name three times. Then, he let himself fall, curled up, like a bundle, the foam splashing high all around him. And the Chanteclair resumed its singing in the weeds.

When the two bodies were found, people assumed there had been a fight, and concocted a whole story. Julien must have been lying in wait for young Colombel, to take revenge on him for his mockeries; and he had thrown himself into the river, after killing him by bashing in his temple with a stone. Three months later, Mlle Thérèse de Marsanne married the young Comte de Véteuil. She was wearing a white dress, her face was beautiful and calm, haughty in its purity.

Nantas

1

The room Nantas had been living in since his arrival from Marseilles was on the top floor of a house in the rue de Lille, next to the residence of Baron Danvilliers, a member of the Council of State. This house belonged to the Baron, who had had it built over some old outhouses. Nantas, if he leant forward, could see a corner of the Baron's garden, which was shaded by some superb trees. Beyond that, over the green treetops, a vista opened up across Paris; you could see the gap where the Seine was, the Tuileries, the Louvre, the line of the river-banks, a whole sea of rooftops, as far as the hazy distance of the Père Lachaise cemetery.

It was a narrow attic room, with a window cut into the slate roof. Nantas had furnished it simply with a bed, a table, and a chair. He had settled down here as he was looking for something cheap, having made up his mind to camp out until he had found some sort of job. The dirty wallpaper, the black ceiling, the poverty and bareness of this cramped room in which there wasn't even a fireplace did not bother him. Ever since he had been able to go to sleep with a view over the Louvre and the Tuileries, he had compared himself to a general, sleeping in some wretched roadside inn, ahead of him the huge and wealthy city that he is to take the following day.

Nantas' story was a short one. He was the son of a Marseilles mason, and had begun his studies at that city's *lycée*, pushed on by the ambitious affection of his mother, who dreamt of making a gentleman of him. His parents had bled themselves dry to get him as far as his baccalaureate. Then, as his mother had died, Nantas was obliged to accept a humble job with a merchant, where for twelve years he led a weary life, the monotony of which drove him to distraction. He would have run away twenty times over if his filial duty had not kept him stuck in Marseilles, near his father who had fallen off some scaffolding and ended up a cripple. Now he had to make enough for all their needs. But one evening, returning home from work, he found the mason dead, his pipe still warm next to him. Three days later, he sold the few old garments in the house, and set off for Paris, with two hundred francs in his pocket.

Nantas was stubbornly ambitious to make his fortune, a desire he had inherited from his mother. He was a young man who made up his mind quickly, and was coldly determined. While still a boy, he described himself as endowed with great strength. People had often laughed at him when he had forgotten himself so far as to confide in them and to repeat his favourite phrase, 'I'm really strong,' a phrase which became comic when you saw him with his slim black frock-coat, coming apart at the shoulders, with his wrists sticking out of the sleeves. Little by little, he had in this way made a religion of strength, seeing it and it alone in the world, convinced that the strong are, after all, the ones who end up the winners. In his opinion, it was enough to want something and to be able to get it. The rest had no importance.

On Sundays, when he went for a solitary stroll through the sun-baked suburbs of Marseilles, he felt he was a genius; in the depths of his being there was as it were an instinctive impulse pushing him onward; and he would return home to eat a mundane plateful of potatoes with his infirm father, telling himself that one day he would surely be able to carve out for himself a share of the goods in that society in which he was still a nobody at thirty years of age. This was no base desire, no craving for vulgar enjoyments; it was the definite feeling of an intelligence and a will-power that, not finding themselves in their right place, intended to rise imperturbably to that place, through a natural and logical necessity.

As soon as he set foot on the streets of Paris, Nantas thought that he would need merely to stretch out his hands to find a position worthy of him. That same day, he launched his campaign. He had been given letters of recommendation that he took to the addresses indicated; in addition, he knocked on the doors of several people from his own region, hoping for their support. But, after a month, he had obtained nothing in the way of results; the time wasn't right, he was told; in other places, people made him promises that they quickly broke. Meanwhile, his meagre purse was getting emptier, he had at most some twenty francs left. And it was off these twenty francs that he had to live for a whole month more, eating nothing other than bread, traipsing round Paris from morning to evening, and coming back to bed, in his room without light, worn-out, always empty-handed. He refused to be discouraged; but a dull anger rose within him. Destiny seemed to him illogical and unjust.

One evening, Nantas returned home without having eaten. The day before, he had finished his last hunk of bread. No money left, and not a friend to lend him twenty sous. Rain had been falling all day long, that grey Paris rain that can be so cold. A river of mud was flowing down the streets. Nantas, soaked to the skin, had been to Bercy, then to Montmartre, where he had been told that jobs were available; but at Bercy the position had been taken, and his handwriting had been considered not neat enough in Montmartre. These were his two last chances. He would have accepted anything at all, certain as he was that he would carve out his fortune once he had landed his first position. All he asked for, to begin with, was bread, enough money to live on in Paris, and a little patch of land on which he could then build stone by stone. From

Montmartre to the rue de Lille he walked slowly, his heart full to the brim with bitterness. The rain had stopped falling, a bustling crowd jostled him on the pavements. He halted for several minutes outside a money changer's: five francs might perhaps have sufficed for him to be one day the master of this whole world; with five francs you can live for a week, and in a week you can do a great many things. As he dreamed on, a carriage splashed him, and he had to wipe his mud-spattered brow. That made him walk more quickly, his teeth clenched, seized by a fierce desire to lash out with his fists at the crowd blocking every street: this would have avenged him for the obtuseness of destiny. An omnibus almost ran over him in the rue Richelieu. Halfway across the Place du Carrousel, he cast an envious glance at the Tuileries. On the Pont des Saints-Pères, a well-dressed little girl obliged him to deviate from the headlong path he was pursuing with all the blind persistence of a boar being hunted by a pack of hounds; and this detour struck him as the ultimate humiliation: even children were getting in his way! Finally, when he had found refuge in his room, like a wounded animal returning to its lair to die, he slumped into his chair, exhausted, examining his trousers stiffened by the dried mud, and his down-at-heel shoes from which a pool of water was leaking out over the tiled floor.

This time it really was the end. Nantas wondered how he would kill himself. His pride was still intact, he reckoned that his suicide would punish Paris. To have such strength, to feel such power within yourself, and not to find a single person who divines your aspirations and can start you off with a few francs! This seemed to him a monstrous absurdity, his entire being rose in anger. Then he was filled with an immense sense of regret, as his eyes fell on his arms hanging at his sides. And yet he was quite undaunted by any task; with the tip of his little finger he could have lifted up a whole world; and there he sat, flung back into his corner, reduced to impotence, like a caged lion gnawing its own paws. But soon he calmed down, deciding that death was more glorious. As a boy, he had been told the story of an inventor who, having constructed a marvellous machine, one day smashed it to pieces with a hammer in response to the indifference of the crowd. Well, he was that man! He harboured within himself an unprecedented strength, a mechanism of rare intelligence and will-power, and he was going to destroy this machine by smashing his skull against the cobbles of the street.

The sun was setting behind the tall trees of the Danvilliers residence, an autumn sun whose golden rays lit up the yellowed leaves. Nantas stood up as if to follow the sun as it bade farewell. He was going to die, he needed light. For a few seconds, he leant out. Often, between the masses of foliage, he had noticed a young blond girl, very tall, walking along as proud as a princess. He was quite unromantic, and had outgrown the age at which young men dream, in their garrets, that the young ladies of the world are heading their way bringing them great passions and great fortunes. And yet it so happened that, at this supreme hour of suicide, he suddenly remembered that beautiful blond girl and her haughty air. What could her name be? But at the same minute he clenched his fists, feeling nothing but hatred for the inhabitants of that great house whose half-open windows partly revealed rooms of a sober elegance, and he murmured in a fit of rage: 'Oh! I'd sell myself, I'd sell myself if only someone would give me the first hundred sous of my future fortune!'

This idea of selling himself absorbed him for a while. If there had been a pawnshop somewhere, where loans were made on will-power and energy, he would have gone to pledge himself. He imagined market-places in which a politician would come and buy him as a useful instrument, or where a banker would pick him up and set his intelligence to work; and he would accept, holding honour in disdain, telling himself he just had to be strong and he would triumph one day. Then, a smile came to his lips. Is it so easy to sell yourself? Rascals on the lookout for every opportunity still die in poverty, without ever being able to lay their hands on a buyer. He was afraid of being a coward, he told himself he was simply inventing distractions. And he sat down again, swearing that he would throw himself out of the window once night had fallen.

However, his fatigue was so great that he went to sleep in his chair. He was abruptly woken by the sound of voices. It was his concierge who was showing a visitor into his room.

'Monsieur,' she began, 'I took the liberty of showing up this lady…'

And, seeing there was no light in the room, she hastily went down to fetch a candle. She seemed to know the person she had brought in, who was both obliging and respectful.

'There,' she continued as she withdrew. 'You can have a chat, no one will bother you.'

Nantas, who had woken with a start, looked at the lady in surprise. She had lifted her veil. She was forty-five, small, very plump, with the chubby white face of a pious old woman. He had never seen her before. When he offered her the sole chair, with an inquisitive glance, she gave her name: 'Mademoiselle Chuin… I have come, monsieur, to discuss an important matter with you.'

He had had to sit down on the edge of the bed. The name Mlle Chuin meant nothing to him. He decided to wait for her to explain herself. But she was in no hurry; she had taken in the cramped room at a single glance, and seemed to be hesitating as to how to launch into the conversation. Finally, she started to speak, very softly, smiling her way through the more delicate bits.

'Monsieur, I come as a friend... I have been given the most touching information concerning you. Don't think for a moment you have been spied on. In all this, there is nothing other than the strong desire to be of some use to you. I know how roughly life has treated you up to now, with what courage you have struggled to find a position, and the disappointing result hitherto of so many efforts... Forgive me again, monsieur, for intruding into your life like this. I swear that sympathy alone...'

Nantas did not interrupt her, overcome by curiosity, thinking that his concierge must have given her all these details. Mlle Chuin was free to continue, and yet she was trying to come up with more and more compliments, seeking flattering ways of conveying her message.

'You're a young man with a great future, monsieur. I have taken the liberty of following your attempts and I have been greatly struck by your commendable firmness in the face of misfortune. And it seems to me that you would go far, if someone held out a helping hand to you.'

She stopped once more. She was waiting for some reply. The young man decided this lady had come to offer him a job. He answered that he would accept anything. But now that the ice was broken, she asked him bluntly: 'Would you have any objection to getting married?'

'Getting married?' exclaimed Nantas. 'Good Lord, who would want me, madame?... Some poor girl I wouldn't even be able to feed.'

'No, a beautiful, rich young girl, of magnificent lineage, who at a stroke will place in your hands the means of arriving at the highest position.'

Nantas stopped laughing.

'So, what's the deal?' he asked, instinctively lowering his voice.

'This girl is pregnant, and the child needs to be acknowledged,' said Mlle Chuin straightforwardly, forgetting her ingratiating turns of phrase so as to get to the heart of the matter more quickly.

Nantas' first impulse was to throw the old bawd out.

'What you're proposing is shameful,' he murmured.

'Oh, shameful is it?' exclaimed Mlle Chuin, reverting to her honeyed tone, 'I can't accept that horrid word… The truth is, monsieur, that you will save a family from despair. The father doesn't know a thing, the pregnancy is still in its first stages; and I'm the one who conceived the idea of marrying off the poor girl as soon as possible, so as to pass the husband off as the child's father. I know the girl's father, it would kill him. My scheme will deaden the blow, he'll take it as a form of reparation… The problem is that the real seducer is married. Ah, monsieur, there are some men who really have no moral sense…'

She could have gone on in this vein for a long time. Nantas was no longer listening. Why, after all, should he refuse? Hadn't he been asking to sell himself just now? Well, someone had come along to buy him. It was a fair exchange. He would give his name, he would get a job in return. It was a contract like any other. He looked at his trousers stained with the mud of Paris, he remembered he hadn't eaten since the day before, all the anger that had been accumulating during those two months of job-seeking and humiliation flooded into his heart.

At last! He was going to trample on that world which rejected him and drove him to suicide!

'I accept,' he said baldly.

Then, he demanded clearer details from Mlle Chuin. What did she want for playing the go-between? She protested she wanted nothing. However, she finally asked for twenty thousand francs, from the marriage portion the young man would be given. And as he declined to haggle, she became expansive.

'Listen, I was the one who thought of you. The young woman didn't say no, when I mentioned your name... Oh, it's a real bargain! you'll thank me later. I could have found a titled gentleman, I know one who would have kissed my hands. But I preferred to go for someone outside the social circles of this poor girl. It will seem more romantic... What's more, I like you. You're nice, you don't have your head in the clouds. Oh! you'll go far. Don't forget me, I am at your service.'

Until then, no name had been mentioned. At a question from Nantas, the old maid stood up and said, introducing herself once more: 'Mademoiselle Chuin... I have been in Baron Danvilliers' household since the death of the Baroness, working as a governess. It is I who brought up Mademoiselle Flavie, the daughter of Monsieur le Baron... Mademoiselle Flavie is the young woman in question.'

And she withdrew, after having discreetly laid on the table an envelope containing a five-hundred-franc note. It was an advance made by her, to meet the first expenses. When he was alone, Nantas went over to the window. The night was very dark; only the clump of trees could be made out by their deeper shade; a window was shining in the dark façade of the Baron's house. So, it was that tall blond girl, who walked with the gait of a queen and who did not deign to notice him. She or another woman, what did it matter now! Women as such didn't come into the equation. Then Nantas lifted his gaze, looking over Paris rumbling in the darkness, over the river, the streets, the crossroads of the Left Bank, lit by dancing gas flames; and he addressed Paris in a newly familiar, almost intimate tone of superiority.

'You're all mine now!'

2

Baron Danvilliers was in the salon that he used as a study, a high, austere room, fitted with antique furniture, and with leather-covered walls. For two days, he had been quite crushed by the story Mlle Chuin had told him of Flavie's disgrace. However much she tried to break the news gently and tone down the facts, the old man had sustained a heavy blow, and only the thought that the seducer could offer a supreme reparation still kept him going. That morning, he was waiting for the visit of this man he had never met and who was taking his daughter from him in this way. He rang.

'Joseph, a young man is coming, you are to show him in… I'm not at home for anyone else.'

And he relapsed into bitter reflections, sitting alone at his fireside. The son of a mason, a starveling who had no job worth the name! Mlle Chuin did, it's true, make him out to be a young man with a future, but how shameful it all was, in a family which had been quite untarnished until then! Flavie had taken all the blame on herself, in a kind of fury of self-accusation, to spare her governess the slightest reproach. Ever since that painful confession, she had kept to her room, the Baron had refused to see her again. He wanted, before forgiving her, to settle this dreadful business himself. He had made all the necessary arrangements. But the rest of his hair had turned white, his head was shaking with infirmity.

'Monsieur Nantas,' announced Joseph.

The Baron did not get up. He simply turned his head and stared at Nantas as he came in. Nantas had had the good sense not to yield to his desire to dress up in brand-new clothes; he had bought a frock-coat and black trousers, all still clean but very threadbare, and this gave him the appearance of a poor, neatly dressed student, with not the slightest hint of a man on the make. He stopped in the middle of the room, and stood waiting, but without any undue humility.

'So it's you, monsieur,' stuttered the old man.

But he was unable to continue, his voice was choked by emotion; he feared he might give way to violence. After a pause, he said simply, 'Monsieur, you have committed a grave offence.'

And, as Nantas was about to apologise, he repeated with greater vigour: 'A grave offence... I just don't want to know anything about it, I beg you not to try and explain it to me. Even if my daughter had flung herself at you, your crime would still be as great... Only thieves manage to break into families like this.'

Nantas had again bowed his head.

'It's a dowry won cheaply, it's an ambush you laid in the certain knowledge that father and daughter would fall into it...'

'Monsieur, allow me...' interrupted the young man, his resentment growing.

But the Baron made a terrible gesture.

'What? What do you want me to allow you to say?... You have no place to be speaking here. I will say what I have to say to you, and you will have to hear, since you come to me as the guilty party... You have insulted me. You see this house, our family has lived here for more than three centuries without a blemish; can you not feel an age-old sense of honour, a tradition of dignity and respect? Well, sir, you have given all that a real slap in the face. I have almost died from the shock, and today my hands are trembling, as if I had suddenly aged ten years... Be quiet and hear me out.'

Nantas had become very pale. The role he had taken on was proving a difficult one. However, he attempted to present the blindness of his passion as an excuse.

'I lost my head,' he murmured, trying to make up a novelistic story. 'I could not see Mademoiselle Flavie...'

At his daughter's name, the Baron rose and cried out in a voice of thunder:

'Be quiet! I told you I just don't want to know. Whether my daughter went running after you, or you came running after her, is no business of mine. I have asked her nothing, and I ask nothing from you. You can both keep your confessions to yourselves, that is a cesspool I have no intention of venturing into.'

He sat down, trembling, exhausted. Nantas bowed, pro-foundly shaken, despite his self-control. After a silence, the old man resumed, in the dry tones of a man doing business: 'I beg your pardon, monsieur. I had sworn I would keep calm. I have no power over you, but you have power over me, since I am at your mercy. You are here to offer me a deal that has become unavoidable. Let us strike that deal, monsieur.'

And he now affected to speak like a solicitor settling out of court some opprobrious lawsuit, which he is handling only with disgust. He said with composure, 'Mademoiselle Flavie Danvilliers inherited, on the death of her mother, a sum of two hundred thousand francs, which was not meant to come into her hands until her wedding day. This sum has already yielded interest. And here, furthermore, are my trusteeship accounts, which I wish you to be apprised of.'

He had opened a dossier, he read out some figures. Nantas tried in vain to stop him. He was now seized with compunction at the sight of this old man, so upright and simple, who seemed to him quite grand, now that he had calmed down.

'Finally,' the latter concluded, 'I agree to give you, in accordance with the contract my lawyer drew up this morning, a marriage portion capital of two hundred thousand francs. I know you have nothing. You will pick up the two hundred thousand francs at my banker's, the day after the wedding.'

'But monsieur,' said Nantas, 'I'm not asking you for your money, I want only your daughter…'

The Baron stopped him in mid-flow.

'You do not have the right to refuse, and my daughter could not possibly marry a man less wealthy than she is… I am giving you the dowry I was intending for her, that is all. Perhaps you had been expecting more, but people think I am richer than I actually am, monsieur.'

And, as the young man remained speechless at this last cruel remark, the Baron brought the interview to a close by ringing for his servant.

'Joseph, tell mademoiselle that I am expecting her straight away in my study.'

He had risen to his feet and uttered not a word more, walking slowly up and down. Nantas continued to stand there motionless. He was deceiving this old man, he felt himself to be small and without strength in comparison. At last, Flavie entered.

'My daughter,' said the Baron, 'here is that man. The marriage will take place within the time allotted by law.'

And he went off, leaving them alone, as if, for him, the marriage was all arranged. Once the door had closed behind him, silence reigned. Nantas and Flavie looked at each other. They had not yet seen each other. She struck him as very beautiful, with her pale, haughty face, whose big grey eyes did not flinch. Perhaps she had been crying for the three days she had not left her room; but the coldness of her cheeks must have frozen her tears. She was the first to speak.

'So, monsieur, this business is settled?'

'Yes, madame,' Nantas replied simply.

Involuntarily, she pulled a face, looking him slowly up and down, as if to detect some sign of his infamy.

'So much the better, then,' she continued. 'I was afraid I might not find anyone prepared for such a deal.'

Nantas sensed in her voice all the contempt in which she held him. But he looked up again. If he had trembled before the father, knowing that he was deceiving him, he intended to be firm and forthright with the daughter, who was his accomplice.

'Excuse me, madame,' he said quietly, with great politeness, 'I believe you misapprehend the situation that involves us both in what you have just called, quite correctly, a deal. I intend that, as from today, we should treat each other as equals...'

'Oh really!' interrupted Flavie with a disdainful smile.

'Yes, as complete equals... You need a name so as to conceal a wrongdoing that I will not presume to judge, and I am giving you mine. On my side, I need an initial capital, a certain social position, to realise the great plans I have, and you are providing me with that capital. From today we are two partners whose business contributions balance out; all that remains is for us to thank each other for the service we are mutually rendering one another.'

She had stopped smiling. There was a furrow of angered pride on her brow. But she did not reply. After a silence, she continued: 'Do you know my conditions?'

'No, madame,' said Nantas, remaining perfectly calm. 'Please be so good as to dictate them to me, and I will comply in advance.'

Then she expressed her wishes clearly, without hesitation or blush.

'You will never be my husband in more than name. Our lives will remain completely distinct and separate. You will abandon every right over me, and I will have no duty towards you.'

At every sentence, Nantas nodded his acceptance. That was exactly what he wanted. He added, 'If I felt obliged to be gallant, I would tell you that such harsh conditions reduce me to despair. But we are above such insipid compliments. I am very happy to see you are brave enough to face up to our respective situations. We are starting out on life by a path that is not strewn with flowers… I ask only one thing of you, madame: not to make use of the freedom I am granting you in such a way as to make it necessary for me to intervene.'

'Monsieur!' said Flavie heatedly, with mutinous pride.

But he bowed respectfully, begging her not to take offence. Their position was delicate, they both had to tolerate certain allusions, without which any proper understanding would become impossible. He avoided insisting any further. Mlle Chuin, in a second interview, had told him the story of Flavie's wrongdoing. Her seducer was a certain M. des Fondettes, the husband of one of her friends from convent school. While spending a month at their country home, she had found herself one evening in this man's arms, without quite knowing how it had happened and to what extent she was a consenting party. Mlle Chuin almost went so far as to call it rape.

Suddenly, Nantas felt more friendly towards her. Like all those aware of their own strength, he liked to be good-natured.

'Look here, madame,' he exclaimed, 'we don't know each other; but it would be quite wrong of us to hate each other like this, at first sight. Perhaps we are made to get along with one another... I can see clearly that you despise me; that's because you don't know the story of my life.'

And he spoke feverishly, working himself up, recounting his life consumed by ambition, in Marseilles, telling her of the rage of his two months of useless exertions in Paris. Then, he showed his disdain for what he called the social conventions, in which ordinary mortals are bogged down. What did the judgement of the mob count for, when you could trample it underfoot! The important thing was to be superior. Supreme power excused everything. And he painted a vivid picture of the splendid life he would be able to make for himself. He no longer feared any obstacle, nothing could prevail against strength. He would be strong, he would be happy.

'Don't think I am motivated by vulgar self-interest,' he added. 'I'm not selling myself for your fortune. I am taking your money simply as a means of getting well ahead in life... Oh, if only you knew everything that's brewing within me, if only you knew the fervid nights I've spent mulling over the same dream, which was swept away by the reality of each new morning, you would understand me, you would perhaps be proud to lean on my arm, telling yourself that you are finally providing me with the means of being someone!'

She stood listening to him bolt upright, not a muscle in her face stirred. And he kept asking himself a question he had been turning over in his mind for the past three days, without being able to find the answer: had she noticed him at his window, since she had accepted so readily Mlle Chuin's plan, when the latter had named him? The strange idea occurred to him that she would perhaps have started to fall romantically in love with him if he had indignantly turned down the deal the governess had come to propose to him.

He fell silent, and Flavie remained icy. Then, as if he had not made his confession to her, she repeated drily, 'So: my husband in name only, our lives completely distinct, absolute freedom.'

Nantas immediately reassumed his ceremonious attitude, the curt tones of a man discussing a treaty.

'Signed and sealed, madame.'

And he withdrew, displeased with himself. How had he managed to succumb to the stupid desire to convince that woman? She was very beautiful, it was better that there should be nothing in common between them since she might prove a nuisance in his life.

3

Ten years had elapsed. One morning, Nantas found himself in the study where Baron Danvilliers had once given him such a rough reception, on their first meeting. Now this study was his; the Baron, after making peace with his daughter and his son-in-law, had handed the house over to them, just keeping for himself a lodge at the other end of the garden, on the rue de Beaune. In ten years, Nantas had ended up winning one of the highest financial and industrial positions. Involved in all the big railway concerns, launched on all the land speculations that were such a feature of the first years of the Second Empire, he had rapidly made a huge fortune. But his ambition did not end there, he wanted to play a role in public life, and he had managed to get himself appointed deputy, in a part of the country where he owned several farms. No sooner had he entered the Legislative Body than he had set himself up as a future finance minister. Through his extraordinary knowledge and his fluency in public speaking, he was daily assuming a greater and greater importance. Furthermore, he astutely showed an absolute devotion to the Empire, whilst holding in financial matters his own personal theories, which caused quite a stir and which he knew greatly preoccupied the Emperor.

That morning, Nantas was up to his neck in work. The huge offices he had set up on the ground floor of the house were filled with tremendous activity. It was a world of employees, some motionless behind their counters, others constantly coming and going, slamming the doors behind them; there was a continual clink of gold, open bags disgorging their contents across the tables, the ceaseless chiming of a cash register which seemed to threaten to drown the streets in the flood of its coins. Then, in the antechamber, there was a jostling throng of supplicants, businessmen, and politicians, all Paris on its knees before his power. Often, great personages would wait there patiently for an hour. And he, sitting at his desk, in touch with the provinces and foreign countries, able with his extended arms to embrace the whole world, was finally realising his old dream of strength, feeling himself to be the intelligent motor of a colossal machine able to move kingdoms and empires.

Nantas rang for the usher who acted as his doorkeeper. He seemed worried.

'Germain,' he asked, 'do you know if madame has returned?'

And, as the usher replied that he didn't know, he ordered

him to ask madame's maid to come down. But Germain stayed put.

'Excuse me, monsieur,' he murmured, 'the President of the Legislative Body is here and he insists on seeing you.'

Then Nantas made a gesture of irritation, saying, 'Very well, show him in, and do what I ordered.'

The day before, on a crucial question relating to the budget, a speech by Nantas had created such an impression that the article under debate had been committed for amendment in the way he had asked. After the session, the rumour had spread that the finance minister was on the verge of resignation, and different groups were already designating the young deputy as his successor. He just shrugged: nothing had been done, he had merely had a meeting with the Emperor on a few special points. However, the visit of the President of the Legislative Body could well be significant. He seemed to shake off the preoccupation that clouded his thoughts, stood up and went over to shake the president's hand.

'Ah, Monsieur le Duc,' he said, 'I must ask you to excuse me. I didn't know you were here... I am really touched, believe me, by the honour you are doing me.'

For a few minutes they made casual conversation, in cordial tones. Then, the president, without saying anything definite, gave him to understand that he was sent by the Emperor to sound him out. Would he accept the finance portfolio, and what would his programme be? He, then, with superb calmness, laid down his conditions. But, behind his impassive expression, a shout of triumph was rising. At last he was climbing the topmost rung, he had reached the pinnacle. One step more and all eyes would be looking up to him. As the president was drawing to a close, saying that he was on his way that minute to see the Emperor to let him have the programme under discussion, a little door giving access to the living quarters opened, and madame's maid appeared.

Nantas, suddenly turning ashen again, did not complete the sentence he was uttering. He went swiftly over to this woman, murmuring, 'Excuse me, Monsieur le Duc…'

And, in a low voice, he cross-questioned her. So, had madame left early? Had she said where she was going? When would she back? The maid answered vaguely, like an intelligent girl unwilling to compromise herself. Having realised the naivety of his interrogations he ended up saying simply, 'As soon as madame returns, tell her I wish to speak to her.'

The president, surprised, had moved over to a window and was looking down into the courtyard. Nantas came over to him, apologising again. But he had lost his calm: he stammered, astonishing the president by the clumsiness of his words.

'Well, I've gone and spoilt my chances,' he could not help saying once the president had gone. 'That's one portfolio I'm not going to get.'

And he remained in a state of disquiet, occasionally flaring up into anger. Several persons were shown in. An engineer had a report to present, announcing enormous profits in a mining concern. A diplomat discussed with him a loan that a neighbouring power wanted to arrange in Paris. Various lackeys filed past in succession, reporting on twenty substantial pieces of business. Finally, he received a large number of his colleagues from the Chamber of Deputies; they all heaped exaggerated praise on the speech he had made the day before. Leaning back in his armchair, he accepted this flattery, without a smile. The clinking of gold could still be heard from the offices next door, a vibration like that of a factory made the walls shake, as if all this jingling gold were being manufactured there. He merely had to pick up a pen to send dispatches whose arrival would have overjoyed or dismayed the markets of Europe; he could prevent or precipitate war, by supporting or opposing the loan he had been told about; he even held the budget of France in his grasp, he would soon know if he would be for or against the Empire. This was his moment of triumph, his hypertrophied personality was turning into the pivot around which a whole world rotated. And yet he could not enjoy this triumph in the way he had promised himself he would. He was overcome by weariness, his mind was elsewhere, jumping at the slightest noise. Whenever a flame – the feverish sign of satisfied ambition – rose to his cheeks, he would suddenly feel himself growing pale, as if, from behind, a cold hand had abruptly touched the nape of his neck.

Two hours had gone by, and Flavie had still not appeared. Nantas summoned Germain and told him to find M. Danvilliers, if the Baron was at home. Once he was alone again, he walked up and down in his study, refusing to see anyone else that day. Little by little, his agitation had grown. It was clear that his wife was meeting someone. She must have renewed her relations with M. des Fondettes, who had been a widower for six months. Of course, Nantas refused to fall prey to jealousy; for ten years, he had strictly observed the treaty he had concluded; nonetheless, he intended, he said, not to seem ridiculous. Never would he allow his wife to compromise his position, making him the butt of everyone's mockery. And his strength was abandoning him, while those feelings of a husband who simply wants to be treated with respect overwhelmed him with such disturbing power that he had never experienced anything like it, even when venturing on his most daring gambles in the early days of his fortune.

Flavie came in, still in her town outfit; she had merely taken off her hat and gloves. Nantas, his voice trembling, told her he would have gone up to her room, if she had let him know she was back. But without sitting down, and looking as pressed for time as a client, she gestured him to get on with it.

'Madame,' he began, 'it has become necessary for us to have a talk... Where did you go this morning?'

The quaver in her husband's voice, and the brutality of his question, took her completely by surprise.

'I went,' she replied coldly, 'exactly where I pleased.'

'Precisely, and that's just what I cannot agree to any more,' he continued, turning very pale. 'You have to remember what I told you, I will never tolerate your using the freedom I am granting you in such a way as to dishonour my name.'

Flavie smiled with sovereign contempt.

'Dishonour your name, monsieur? but that's your business, it's a task which has already been accomplished.'

Then, Nantas, driven out of his mind, bore down on her as if he wanted to hit her, stammering, 'Wretched woman, you are coming from the arms of Monsieur des Fondettes... You have a lover, I know it.'

'You're wrong,' she said without recoiling from his threatening posture, 'I've never seen Monsieur des Fondettes again... But even if I did have a lover, that would be no reason for you to reproach me. What difference would it make to you? You're forgetting our agreement, it seems.'

He looked at her for a few moments, wild-eyed; then, shaken with sobs, putting into his cry all the passion he had kept bottled up for so long, he collapsed at her feet.

'Oh Flavie, I love you!'

She, standing erect, pulled away, as he had touched the hem of her dress. But the unhappy man dragged himself after her on his knees, his hands held out.

'I love you, Flavie, I love you like a madman... It just happened, I don't know how. It started years ago. And little by little it has completely vanquished me. Oh I've struggled, I felt this passion was unworthy of me, I remembered our first meeting... But today, I am suffering too much, I have to talk to you...'

He carried on like this for a long time. All his beliefs had broken down. This man who had placed his faith in strength, who maintained that will-power is the only lever capable of moving the world, was reduced to nothing, weak as a child, disarmed before a woman. And now that his dreams of fortune were realised, his high position achieved, he would have given anything for this woman to lift him to his feet and plant a kiss on his brow. She was ruining his moment of triumph. He was deaf, now, to the chime of gold in his offices, he spared not a thought for the parade of courtiers who had just been to pay him homage, he forgot that the Emperor, at this very moment, was perhaps summoning him to high office. These things did not exist. He had everything, and all he wanted was Flavie. If Flavie refused to give herself, he had nothing.

'Listen,' he continued, 'what I did, I did for you... To begin with, it's true, you didn't count, I worked to satisfy my pride. Later, you became the sole object of all my thoughts, all my efforts. I told myself I had to rise as high as possible so as to deserve you. I hoped to make you change your mind the day I placed my power at your feet. See where I am today. Haven't I earned your forgiveness? Don't despise me any longer, I beg of you!'

She had not yet spoken a word. She said calmly, 'Stand up, monsieur, someone might come in.'

He refused, continuing to implore her. Perhaps he would have waited longer, if he hadn't been jealous of M. des

Fondettes. This was a source of torment, driving him mad. Then, he took a very humble tack.

'I can easily see that you still despise me. All right, wait, don't give your love to anyone. I promise you such great things that I'll succeed in making you change your mind. You must forgive me if I was brutal just now. I feel I'm losing my head... Oh, let me hope you'll love me one day!'

'Never!' she said resolutely.

And, as he lay there on the ground, crushed, she tried to leave. But he, beside himself, overcome with rage, leapt up and seized her by the wrists. As if a woman could defy him like this, when the whole world was at his feet! He could do anything, topple entire states, lead France as he wished – and to think he couldn't win his wife's love! He, so strong, so powerful, he whose least wishes were others' commands, had only one desire left, and this desire would never be fulfilled, because this creature, as weak as a child, refused! He gripped her by the arms, repeating hoarsely:

'I want... I want –'

'And I don't want,' Flavie was saying, all white and stiff-necked in her pride.

They were still struggling when Baron Danvilliers opened the door. Seeing him, Nantas let go of Flavie and exclaimed, 'Monsieur, here is your daughter, fresh from her lover's arms... Tell her a wife must respect her husband's name, even if she doesn't love him and the thought of her own honour isn't enough to stop her.'

The Baron, who had aged considerably, stood on the threshold surveying this violent scene. It came as a painful surprise to him. He thought the household was harmonious, and admired the ceremonious relations between husband and wife, thinking they were simply keeping up the proprieties.

His son-in-law and he came from two different generations; but even if his susceptibilities were hurt by the financier's somewhat unscrupulous activities, and he was critical of certain ventures which he described as reckless, he had had to recognise the strength of his will and his lively intelligence. And now, all at once, he was stumbling into this drama of which he had no inkling.

When Nantas accused Flavie of having a lover, the Baron, who still treated his married daughter with the strictness he had shown her at the age of ten, stepped forward with all the solemnity of his age.

'I swear to you that she has just been with her lover,' Nantas repeated, 'and you can see how she stands there and defies me!'

Flavie, disdainfully, was looking away. She smoothed down her cuffs, which her husband's brutality had ruffled. Not a blush had come to her cheeks. But her father turned to address her.

'My daughter, why don't you defend yourself? Could your husband be telling the truth? Could you have kept this one last grief in store for my old age?... The affront would then be for me too; for in a family, the wrongdoing of a single member is enough to sully all the others.'

Then she made a gesture of impatience. Her father was certainly taking his time to accuse her! For a moment longer, she put up with his questioning, wanting to spare him the shame of a quarrel. But, as he in turn lost his temper, seeing her mute and provocative, she finally said, 'Oh come on, Father, let this man play his role... You don't know him. Don't force me to speak, out of respect for you.'

'He is your husband,' resumed the old man. 'He is the father of your child.'

Flavie had drawn herself to her full height, quivering.

'No, no, he is not the father of my child… It's time I told you everything. This man isn't even a seducer, for that at least would have been an excuse, if he had loved me. This man simply sold himself and consented to cover for another man's wrongdoing.'

The Baron turned to Nantas who, whey-faced, was shrinking back.

'Listen, Father!' continued Flavie more forcefully, 'he sold himself, sold himself for money… I have never loved him, he has never so much as laid a finger on me… I wanted to spare you a great grief, I bought his services so he'd lie to you… Look at him, see if I'm telling the truth.'

Nantas was hiding his face in his hands.

'And today,' the young woman continued, 'he comes telling me he even expects me to love him… He fell to his knees and burst into tears. All an act, I'm sure. Forgive me for having deceived you, Father; but do I really belong to that man?… Now that you know everything, take me away. He assaulted me just now, I'm not staying here a moment longer.'

The Baron straightened up his bent figure. And in silence he went over and gave his arm to his daughter. Together they crossed the room, without Nantas making a move to hold them back. Then, at the door, the old man deigned to say simply, 'Goodbye, monsieur.'

The door had closed. Nantas was left alone, crushed, looking wildly at the emptiness all around him. As Germain had just entered and placed a letter on his desk, he opened it mechanically and ran his eyes over it. This letter, entirely handwritten by the Emperor, was offering him, in the most flattering terms, the finance ministry. He barely understood. The realisation of all his ambitions no longer affected him. On the cash desks next door, the clink of gold had grown louder; it was the hour at which Nantas' business house hummed with activity, setting a whole world in motion. And he, in the midst of this colossal labour that was all his creation, at the pinnacle of his power, his eyes gazing stupefied at the Emperor's handwriting, wailed like a child, as if to revoke all he had so far lived through and achieved.

'I'm so unhappy... I'm so unhappy...'

He wept, his head resting on his desk, and his hot tears blotted out the letter appointing him minister.

4

In the eighteen months since Nantas had been appointed finance minister, he seemed to have distracted himself from his sorrows through a superhuman amount of work. The day after the violent scene that had taken place in his study, he had had an interview with Baron Danvilliers; and, on her father's advice, Flavie had agreed to return to the conjugal home. But husband and wife were no longer speaking to each other, apart from the charade they had to put on in society. Nantas had decided that he would not leave his residence. In the evening he would bring his secretaries with him and carry out his tasks at home.

This was the period in his life when he achieved the greatest things. A voice repeatedly inspired him with lofty and fertile ideas. Wherever he went, a murmur of liking and admiration greeted him. But he remained indifferent to all praise. He gave the impression of labouring without hope of any reward, with the intention of amassing his achievements in sole view of attempting the impossible. Each time he rose higher, he scrutinised Flavie's face. Was she touched, at last? Did she forgive him his former infamy, seeing only how much his intelligence had developed? And still he could detect no sign of emotion on that woman's mute face, and he told himself, as he settled back down to his work, 'Come on! I'm still not high enough for her, I have to rise even higher, rise without stopping.' He intended to win through to happiness by sheer strength, just as it was by strength that he had made his fortune. All his belief in his own strength came back to him, he refused to accept that there was any other lever in this world, since it is the desire for life which has made humanity what it is. When at times he fell prey to despondency, he would lock himself away so no one would suspect the weaknesses of his flesh. His struggles could be surmised only from his increasingly deep-set, dark-rimmed eyes, in which an intense flame was burning.

He was now consumed by jealousy. To have failed to make Flavie love him was torture; but he was enraged and maddened at the thought that she could give herself to another man. To assert her freedom, she was capable of showing herself in public with M. des Fondettes. So he affected to take no notice of her, while in fact enduring agonies of anguish at her slightest absence. If he had not been afraid of appearing ridiculous, he would have followed her along the streets himself. It was then that the idea came to him of having her shadowed by a person whose loyalty he would buy.

Mlle Chuin had been kept on in the house. The Baron was used to her. In any case, she knew too much for them to get rid of her. The old maid had briefly planned to retire with the twenty thousand francs that Nantas had allotted her, the day after his wedding. But doubtless she had told herself that the house was a place in whose murky waters it might be profitable for her to fish. So she was on the lookout for a new opportunity, having calculated that she still needed twenty thousand francs or so, if she wanted to buy, back in Roinville, where she came from, the lawyer's house that she had so admired in her youth.

Nantas did not need to stand on ceremony with this old maid, whose expressions of sugary piety could no longer fool him. Still, on the morning he summoned her into his study and openly proposed that she keep him informed of his wife's least activities, she pretended to protest, asking him whom he took her for.

'Oh come now, mademoiselle,' he said impatiently, 'I'm a busy man, I've got people waiting. Let's not beat about the bush, please.'

But she refused to listen to another word, unless he respected certain proprieties. She was a woman of principle who thought that things are not fair or foul in themselves, but become so depending on how they are presented.

'Very well,' he continued, 'it's a good deed that I have in mind, mademoiselle... I am afraid my wife may be hiding some anxieties from me. She has been looking sad for several weeks now, and I thought of you as someone who could find out why.'

'You can count on me,' she said, with maternal effusiveness. 'I am devoted to madame, I will do anything for her honour and yours... Starting tomorrow, we'll keep an eye on her.'

He promised to reward her for her services. At first she was indignant. Then, she cleverly forced him to name a sum: he would give her ten thousand francs, if she could give him formal proof of madame's good or bad behaviour. Little by little, they had eventually managed to come down to specifics.

Thereafter, Nantas tormented himself less. Three months went by, he found himself engrossed in a huge task, the preparation of the budget. In agreement with the Emperor, he had made important modifications to the financial system. He knew he would be bitterly attacked in the Chamber of Deputies, and it was necessary for him to prepare a considerable number of documents. Often he would work all through the night. That deadened his feelings and gave him patience. Whenever he saw Mlle Chuin, he would interrogate her briskly. Did she know anything? Had madame been out visiting a lot? Had she stayed particularly long in certain houses? Mlle Chuin kept a detailed diary. But so far she had picked up only unimportant facts. Nantas was starting to feel reassured, while the old woman sometimes winked, repeating that soon, perhaps, she would have some news.

The truth was that Mlle Chuin had thought long and hard. Ten thousand francs wasn't going to be enough for her, she needed twenty thousand if she was going to buy the lawyer's house. At first she had the idea of selling herself to the wife, after selling herself to the husband. But she knew madame, and was afraid she'd be turned out at the first word she uttered. For a long time, even before she had been given this particular task, she had been spying on madame on her own account, telling herself that the vices of the masters can make fortunes for their servants; and she had come up against one of those characters whose honesty is all the more impregnable as it is built on a sense of pride. Flavie's wrongdoing had left her with a grudge against all men. So Mlle Chuin was starting to despair, when one day she met M. des Fondettes. He questioned her so avidly about her mistress that she suddenly realised that he was madly lusting after her, inflamed by the memory of the minute he had held her in his arms. And her plan was settled: she would serve both the husband and the lover – a scheme of genius, she thought.

Everything, indeed, came together just as she wanted. M. des Fondettes, rejected, deprived of hope, would have given his fortune to possess once more that woman who had been his. He was the first to sound out Mlle Chuin. He saw her again, put on a show of emotion, swearing that he would kill himself if she didn't help him. At the end of a week, after a great display of sensibility and scruples, the deal was struck: he would give ten thousand francs, and she, one evening, would hide him in Flavie's room.

In the morning, Mlle Chuin went to see Nantas.

'What have you found out?' he asked, turning pale.

But at first she wouldn't go into details. Madame was certainly having an affair. She was even letting someone come to her apartment.

'Get to the point, get to the point,' he repeated, furious with impatience.

Finally, she named M. des Fondettes.

'This evening, he's going to be in madame's room.'

'That's fine, thank you,' stammered Nantas.

He gestured her to leave, afraid he might faint in front of her. This brusque dismissal came as a most pleasant surprise to her, as she had been expecting a long interrogation, and she had even prepared her answers in advance, so as not to get confused. She curtseyed, and withdrew, assuming a doleful expression.

Nantas had risen to his feet. As soon as he was by himself, he spoke out loud.

'This evening... In her room...'

And he held his hands to his skull, as if he had heard it cracking open. This meeting, arranged in the conjugal house, seemed to him a monstrous piece of impudence. He could not let himself be insulted in this way. His wrists were clenched like those of a wrestler, his rage inspired him with dreams of murder. But he had a piece of work to finish. Three times he sat back down at his desk, and three times his whole body rebelled, forcing him to his feet, while, from behind him, something urged him on, a need to go up immediately to his wife's apartment and tell her she was a trollop. Finally he mastered himself, he settled back to his task, swearing that he would strangle them that evening. This was the greatest victory he ever won over himself.

That afternoon, Nantas went to the Emperor to submit the final draft of the budget. When the latter put forward a few objections, he went through them with perfect lucidity. But he had to promise to modify a whole section of his work. The bill had to be brought in the following day.

'Sire, I'll stay up all night,' he said.

And, on his way home, he thought, 'I'll kill them at midnight, and then I'll have until daybreak to finish this task.'

That evening, over dinner, Baron Danvilliers talked about this very same draft budget, which was giving rise to a lot of speculation. He did not approve of all his son-in-law's ideas when it came to financial matters, but he found them wide-ranging and quite remarkable. As he was replying to the Baron, Nantas on several occasions thought he caught his wife's eyes fixed on his. Often, these days, she would gaze at him in this way. Her gaze showed no emotion, she was simply listening to him and seemed to be trying to read what was hidden behind his expression. Nantas thought that she was afraid she had been betrayed. So he made an effort to appear as casual as he could: he talked a great deal, rose to heights of eloquence, and ended up convincing his father-in-law, who yielded to his great intelligence. Flavie was still gazing at him; and a scarcely perceptible ripple of softness had swept momentarily across her face.

Until midnight, Nantas worked in his study. He had gradually become more and more enthralled by his task, nothing else existed but this creation of his, this financial mechanism which he had slowly constructed, cog by cog, in the face of innumerable obstacles. When the clock struck midnight, he instinctively looked up. A deep silence prevailed through the house. Suddenly he remembered: adultery was at large, there in the depths of that shadow and silence. But he found it painful to have to get up out of his chair: he regretfully laid down his pen, took a few steps as if to obey an old desire which he no longer felt. Then his face flushed hot, his eyes glowed with fire. And he went up to his wife's apartment.

That evening, Flavie had sent her maid away early. She wanted to be alone. Until midnight, she remained in the little salon that led to her bedroom. Stretched out on a love-seat, she had picked up a book; but every minute the book would fall from her hands, and she would daydream, her eyes staring vacantly. Her face had grown softer again, from time to time a pallid smile passed over it.

She sat up with a start. There had been a knock at the door. 'Who is it?'

'Open the door,' replied Nantas.

It was such a great surprise for her that she opened the door automatically. Never before had her husband turned up at her apartment like this. He came in, in a real state; anger had overcome him again as he was climbing the stairs. Mlle Chuin, who had been watching out for him on the landing, had just murmured in his ear that M. des Fondettes had been there for two hours. So he did not mince his words.

'Madame,' he said, 'there is a man hidden in your room.'

Flavie did not reply at once, her thoughts were so distracted. Finally she understood.

'You are crazy, monsieur,' she murmured.

But, without stopping to argue, he was already walking towards the bedroom. Then, she leapt in front of the door, shouting, 'You're not going in… I am in my own home here, and I forbid you to go in!'

Quivering, seeming taller than usual, she blocked the door. For a moment they stood there, motionless, without a word, staring straight into each other's eyes. He, his neck straining, his hands outstretched, was about to throw himself on her and force his way past.

'Get out of my way,' he murmured hoarsely. 'I'm stronger than you, I'll get in whether you like it or not.'

'No you won't, I won't let you.'

Frenziedly he repeated, 'There's a man in there, there's a man in there…'

She, not even deigning to deny his accusation, shrugged. Then, as he took another step forward: 'All right! Say there is a man in there, what's it got to do with you? Aren't I free?'

He recoiled at that word which stung him like a slap in the face. She was indeed free. A cold chill took him by the shoulders, he felt clearly that she had the superior role and that he was playing the part of a sick and illogical child. He wasn't observing the treaty, his stupid passion was making him hateful. Why hadn't he stayed in his study, working? The blood drained from his cheeks, his face turned the dark ashen hue of unspeakable suffering. When Flavie noticed the depth of his emotion, she moved away from the door, while her eyes grew softer and more tender.

'See,' she said simply.

And she herself went into the room, holding a lamp, while

Nantas remained in the doorway. He had gestured to her, saying it was useless, that he didn't want to see. But she was now the one to insist. As she came up to the bed, she lifted the curtains, and M. des Fondettes appeared, hiding behind them. She was so stupefied by this that she cried out in horror.

'It's true', she stammered, distraught, 'it's true, this man was here... I didn't know, oh! on my life I swear it!'

Then, making an effort of will, she calmed down, she even seemed to regret this first instinct which had just driven her to defend herself.

'You were right, monsieur, and I ask your pardon,' she said to Nantas, trying to find her usual cold voice.

But meanwhile, M. des Fondettes was feeling ridiculous. He looked a real fool, he would have given a great deal for the husband to lose his temper. But Nantas remained silent. He had simply gone very pale. When he had turned his gaze from M. des Fondettes back to Flavie, he bowed to the latter, uttering this one sentence: 'Madame, forgive me, you are free.'

And he turned round and walked away. In him, something had just broken; only the machinery of his muscles and bones was still functioning. When he found himself back in his study, he walked straight over to a drawer where he kept a revolver hidden. After examining this weapon, he said aloud, as if making a formal arrangement with himself: 'Right, that's enough, I'll kill myself a little later.'

He turned up the flickering lamp, sat down at his desk and calmly set to work again. Without a hesitation, in the middle of the great silence, he continued the sentence he had started. One by one, methodically, the pages piled up. Two hours later, when Flavie, who had sent M. des Fondettes away, came down barefoot to listen at the study door, she could hear nothing but the faint scratching of pen on paper. Then she bent down and put her eye to the keyhole. Nantas was still writing with the same tranquillity, his face expressed the peace and satisfaction of work, while a ray from the lamp lit up the barrel of the revolver next to him.

5

The house adjacent to the garden of the residence was now the property of Nantas, who had bought it from his father-in-law. On a whim, he had forbidden the narrow garret to be let, the one in which he had spent two months struggling against poverty when he first arrived in Paris. Since making his huge fortune, he had, on several occasions, felt the need to go and shut himself away up there for a few hours. It was there he had suffered, it was there he wanted to triumph. Whenever an obstacle got in his way, he also liked to go there to reflect, to take the great decisions of his life. There he could revert to the person he had been before. And so, faced with the necessity of suicide, it was in this garret that he had resolved to die.

It was only at about eight o'clock in the morning that Nantas had finished his work. Afraid that weariness might make him drowsy, he washed himself with plenty of cold water. Then, he summoned several employees in succession, to give them orders. When his secretary had arrived, he talked things over with him: the secretary was to take the draft budget straight away to the Tuileries, and provide certain explanations if the Emperor were to raise further objections. After that, Nantas thought he had done enough. He was leaving everything in good order, he would not be departing like a bankrupt man in a fit of frenzy. He was master of himself, in the final tally, he could do what he wanted with himself, without being accused of egoism and cowardice.

Nine o'clock struck. It was time. But, as he was about to leave his study, taking the revolver with him, he had one last bitter draught to drain. Mlle Chuin turned up to claim the ten thousand francs he had promised her. He paid her, and had to endure her familiarity. She adopted a maternal tone, treating him rather as if he were a successful pupil. If he had still been hesitating, this shameful complicity would have made him resolve on suicide. He went swiftly upstairs and, in his haste, left the key in the door.

Nothing had changed. The wallpaper was still torn in the same places, the bed, the table, and the chair were still there, with their old smell of poverty. For a moment he breathed in that air which reminded him of his struggles of former times. Then, he went across to the window and had the same vista over Paris, the trees of the residence, the Seine, the river-banks, a whole stretch of the right bank, along which the torrent of houses unfurled, rising and then fading away into the distance where the Père Lachaise cemetery lay.

The revolver was on the rickety table, within reach. Now he was no longer in such a hurry, he was certain that no one would come and he would be able to kill himself as and when he wanted. He grew reflective, and told himself that he was at the same point as once long ago – he had been brought back to the same place, with the same desire to kill himself. One evening, once already, right here, he had wanted to dash his brains out; he was too poor then to afford a pistol, he had only the cobbled street, but death was waiting for him down there just the same. And so, in life, only death never deceived you, showing itself ever ready and ever reliable. Death was the only thing he could count on, however hard he had looked, everything else had continually crumbled away beneath him, death alone remained a certainty. And he was filled with regret at having lived ten years too long. The experience he had had of life, on his upward path to fortune and power, seemed to him puerile. What was the use of that expenditure of will-power, what was the use of all that strength he had developed, since, obviously, will and strength were not everything? It had taken just a single passion to destroy him, he had stupidly fallen in love with Flavie, and the monument he was erecting started to crack, and came tumbling down like a house of cards, blown over by the breath of a child. It was a wretched situation, it was like the punishment of a schoolboy stealing fruit, discovering that the branch is breaking beneath him, and dying for his crime by the same means he had used to commit it. Life was absurd, superior men came to the same banal end as idiots.

Nantas had picked the revolver up from the table and started slowly to load it. One last regret made him soften for a second, at this supreme moment. How many great things he would have achieved if Flavie had understood him! The day she flung her arms about his neck, telling him, 'I love you!', would be the day he found a lever to move the world. And his final thought was one of great disdain for strength, since strength, which was supposed to give him everything, had not given him Flavie.

He lifted his weapon. It was a splendid morning. Through the wide-open window the sun shone in, spreading a sense of youthful awakening through the garret. In the distance, Paris was settling down to the labours of a gigantic city. Nantas pressed the barrel of the pistol to his temple.

But the door had been flung violently open, and Flavie entered. She swiftly turned aside the shot, the bullet lodged in the ceiling. The two gazed at each other. She was so out of breath, so choked, that she could not speak. Finally, addressing Nantas with familiarity and affection for the very first time, she came out with the words he was waiting for, the only ones capable of persuading him to live: 'I love you!' she cried, flinging her arms round his neck, sobbing, and wresting this confession from her broken pride, from her entire being, vanquished at last, 'I love you because you're strong!'

Fasting

1

When the curate went up into the pulpit, wearing his broad surplice – angelic in its whiteness – the little Baroness was sitting blissfully in her customary place, near a hot-air vent, next to the chapel of the Holy Angels.

After the usual moment of recollection, the curate delicately passed a fine cambric handkerchief over his lips; then, he opened his arms, like a seraph about to take flight, bent his head, and spoke. His voice was at first, in the vast nave, like a distant murmur of running water, like the amorous plaint of the wind amid the foliage. And, little by little, the low sounds grew louder, the breeze turned into a tempest, the voice rolled round the vaults with the majestic rumble of thunder. But now and again, even in the midst of his most formidable thunderbolts, the curate's voice would keep growing suddenly gentle, shedding a clear ray of sunlight across the dark hurricane of his eloquence.

The little Baroness, at the sound of the first whisperings amid the leaves, had adopted the greedy, spellbound posture of someone with a delicate sense of hearing preparing to savour all the subtleties of a well-loved symphony. She appeared ravished by the exquisite softness of the musical phrases at the beginning; then she followed, with the attention of a connoisseur, the swelling voice and the way the final storm broke out, so cunningly contrived; and when the voice had risen to its maximum volume, when its thunder was magnified by the echoes of the nave, the little Baroness was unable to repress a discreet bravo, nodding her head with satisfaction.

At that moment she was flooded with a heavenly ecstasy. All the devout ladies were swooning.

2

But the curate had something to say, too; his music was there as an accompaniment to his words. He was giving a sermon on fasting, he was saying how pleasing to God were the mortifications of the creature. Leaning against the edge of the pulpit, in the posture of a great white bird, he was sighing: 'The hour has come, my brothers and sisters, in which we must all, like Jesus, carry our cross, crown ourselves with thorns, climb up to our calvary, barefoot among the rocks and brambles.'

The little Baroness doubtless found the phrase smoothly moulded, for she blinked gently as if her heart-strings had been tickled. Then, as the curate's symphony lulled her, while she continued to follow the melodic phrases, she let herself drift into a half-dreaming state filled with intimate voluptuousness.

Opposite her, she could see one of the tall chancel windows, grey with fog. It was evidently still raining. The poor girl had braved some dreadful weather to come to the sermon. You have to suffer a bit for your religion. Her coachman had got thoroughly drenched, and she herself, as she jumped down onto the cobbles, had got her toes slightly wet. Her coupé, it was true, was excellent, sealed and padded like an alcove. But it's so sad to see, through the streaming windows, a line of umbrellas scurrying along every pavement! And she reflected that if the weather had been fine, she would have been able to come in a victoria. That would have been much jollier.

Basically, her main worry was that the curate might dispatch his sermon too quickly. Then she'd have to wait for her carriage, for she would certainly not put up with splashing about in weather like this. And she calculated that, at his present rate, the curate would never have enough voice to keep going for two hours; her coachman would arrive too late. This anxiety somewhat spoilt her pious raptures.

3

The curate, with sudden outbursts of wrath that made him stand upright, his hair unkempt, clenching his fists, like a man in prey to the spirit of vengeance, was threatening:

'And above all, woe unto you, sinful women, if you do not shed on the feet of Jesus Christ the perfume of your remorse, the sweet-smelling balm of your repentance. Believe what I am telling you – tremble, and fall to your knees on the stones. Only if you come to seclude yourselves in the purgatory of penitence, thrown open by the Church during these days of universal contrition; only if you wear away the stone slabs beneath brows made pale by fasting, and sink into the anguish of hunger and cold, of silence and night, will you deserve divine forgiveness, on the glorious day of victory!'

The little Baroness, startled out of her preoccupations by this terrible explosion, slowly and gently nodded her head, as if she entirely agreed with the wrathful curate. You had to take birch rods, withdraw to some really dark, damp, ice-cold corner, and there lash yourself; there was no doubt about it, she thought.

Then she drifted back into her daydreams; she became absorbed in a deep sense of well-being, of yielding ecstasy. She was sitting comfortably on a low broad-backed chair, and under her feet she had an embroidered cushion, which stopped her feeling the cold from the stone slab. Half reclining, she took pleasure in the church, that great vessel in which wisps of incense were floating and whose mysterious, shadowy depths were filled with adorable visions. The nave, with its red velvet hangings, its gold and marble decorations, its atmosphere of a huge boudoir full of disturbing fragrances, lit by the gentle gleam of night-lights, closeted and seemingly ready to be the scene of superhuman love, had little by little enveloped her in the magic of its solemnity. It was a feast for her senses. Her plump, pretty body abandoned itself, stroked, cradled, caressed. And her pleasure came, above all, from feeling herself so small in such a great beatitude.

But, without her being aware of it, what was really tickling her so deliciously was the warm breath of the hot-air vent open almost right under her skirts. The little Baroness was really sensitive to the cold. The air vent discreetly breathed its hot caresses from top to bottom of her silk stockings. She started to drowse, bathing in this soft smooth warmth.

4

The curate was still waxing wrathful. He was plunging all the devout ladies present into the boiling oil of hell.

'If you do not heed the voice of God, if you do not heed my voice which is that of God himself, verily I say unto you, one day you will hear your bones cracking with anguish, you will feel your flesh splitting open over burning coals, and then it will be in vain that you will cry, "Have pity, Lord, have pity, I repent!" God will be merciless, and with his foot he will spurn you deep into the pit of hell!'

At this last sally there was a shudder in the audience. The little Baroness, who was definitely being lulled into somnolence by the hot air playing around her skirts, smiled vacantly. Our little Baroness was well acquainted with the curate. The evening before, he had dined at her house. He loved salmon pâté with truffles, and Pommard was his favourite wine. He was, to be sure, a handsome man, thirty-five to forty years old, with brown hair, and a face so round and pink that you could easily have mistaken his priestly countenance for the merry face of a servant-girl on a farm. What's more, he was a man of the world, a hearty eater with a ready tongue. Women adored him, the Baroness was crazy about him. He would tell her in such adorably honeyed tones: 'Ah, madame, dressed in your finery like that, you're enough to damn a saint!'

And the dear man didn't get himself damned. He would run round to the countess and the Marquise and his other penitent magdalens and spout the same gallantries, which made him the spoiled child of all those ladies.

When he went to dine at the little Baroness' on Thursdays, she would fuss over him as a dear creature who might catch cold at the slightest draught, and who would infallibly get indigestion if a morsel of his food wasn't just right. In the salon, his armchair was placed right next to the fireplace; at table, the servers had been given orders to keep particular watch over his plate, to pour out for him alone a certain twelve-year-old Pommard, which he drank eyes closed with fervour, as if taking communion.

The curate was so nice, so very nice! While from up in his pulpit he was talking of bones cracking and limbs roasting, the little Baroness, half asleep as she was, saw him at her table, blissfully wiping his lips, telling her, 'My dear madame, this is a bisque which would ensure you found grace in the sight of God the Father, if your beauty were not already sufficient for you to be certain of a place in paradise.'

5

The curate, having resorted to anger and threats, began to sob. This was his habitual tactic. Almost on his knees in the pulpit, with only his shoulders visible, then, all at once, rising to his feet and bending forward as if overcome by sorrow, he would wipe his eyes, with a great rustle of starched muslin, he would throw out his arms to right and left, adopting the pose of a wounded pelican. This was the crowning piece, the grand finale for full orchestra, the wild, climactic denouement.

'Weep, weep,' he whimpered, his voice failing; 'weep for yourselves, weep for me, weep for God...'

The little Baroness was completely asleep, her eyes still open. The heat, the incense, the deepening shadows, had quite numbed her. She had curled up into a cocoon, wrapped in the voluptuous sensations she was feeling; and, in this snug secrecy, she was dreaming of the most delightful things.

Next to her, in the chapel of the Holy Angels, there was a big fresco, depicting a group of handsome, half-naked young men, with wings growing out of their backs. They were smiling the smiles of bashful lovers, while their postures, bowing or kneeling, seemed to be adoring some invisible little Baroness. What handsome boys, sweet lips, satin-smooth skin, muscular arms! The worst of it was that one of them was the absolute image of the young Duke of P***, one of the Baroness' good friends. As she dozed, she wondered if the Duke would look good naked, with wings growing out of his back. And, at times, she imagined that the big pink cherub was wearing the Duke's black tails. Then, the dream grew clear: it really was the Duke, in a very short frock-coat, who, from out of the darkness, was blowing her kisses.

6

When the little Baroness awoke, she heard the curate's voice pronouncing the sacramental words: 'And it is grace that I wish you.'

For a few moments she was overcome with surprise; she

thought the curate was wishing her the young Duke's kisses.

There was a great scraping of chairs. Everyone left; the little Baroness had guessed quite correctly, her coachman was not yet waiting at the foot of the steps. That devil of a curate had dispatched his sermon very rapidly, robbing his penitent ladies of at least twenty minutes of eloquence.

And as the little Baroness waited impatiently in a side aisle, she met the curate bustling out of the sacristy. He was looking at his watch, with the hurried air of a man anxious not to miss an appointment.

'Ah, how late I am, dear madame!' he said. 'You know, I'm expected at the Countess'. There's a concert of sacred music, followed by a light meal.'

BIOGRAPHICAL NOTE

Emile Zola was born in April 1840 and grew up in Aix-en-Provence, where he befriended the artist, Paul Cézanne. In 1858, Zola moved to Paris with his mother. Despite her hopes that he would become a lawyer, he in fact failed his baccalaureate, and went on to work for the publisher Hachette, and to write literary columns and art reviews. He lost his job at Hachette on publication of his autobiographical novel, *La Confession de Claude* (1865), before his earliest venture into naturalistic fiction, *Thérèse Raquin* (1867). His series of over twenty volumes, *Les Rougon-Macquart* (1871–93) is a natural and social history of one family under the Second Empire in France, individual volumes exploring social ills and the influence of nature and nurture on human behaviour. *L'Assommoir* (1877) concerned drunkenness and the Parisian working-classes, *Nana* (1880) addressed sexual exploitation, and *Germinal* (1885) considered labour conditions. Other novel sequences followed, always entailing vast amounts of research.

Zola's later life as a writer was famously punctuated by his involvement in the Dreyfus affair, in which a Jewish army officer was falsely accused of selling military secrets to the Germans. In a newspaper letter entitled 'J'Accuse' (1898), Zola challenged the establishment and invited his own trial for libel, the author later removing briefly to England to escape the subsequent prison sentence. Emile Zola died in 1902, apparently asphyxiated by carbon monoxide fumes when asleep. Naturalism declined after his death, but his depictions of 'Nature seen through a temperament' were an important influence on writers such as Theodore Dreiser and August Strindberg.

Andrew Brown studied at the University of Cambridge, where he taught French for many years. He now works as a freelance teacher and translator. He is the author of *Roland Barthes: the Figures of Writing* (OUP, 1993), and his translations include *Memoirs of a Madman* by Gustave Flaubert, *The Jinx* by Théophile Gautier, *Mademoiselle de Scudéri* by E.T.A. Hoffmann, *Theseus* by André Gide, *Incest* by Marquis de Sade, *The Ghost-seer* by Friedrich von Schiller, *Colonel Chabert* by Honoré de Balzac, *Memoirs of an Egotist* by Stendhal, *Butterball* by Guy de Maupassant, *With the Flow* by Joris-Karl Huysmans, *Life of Castruccio Castracani* by Machiavelli, and *A Fantasy of Dr Ox* by Jules Verne, all published by Hesperus Press.

HESPERUS PRESS – 100 PAGES

Hesperus Press, as suggested by the Latin motto, is committed to bringing near what is far – far both in space and time. Works written by the greatest authors, and unjustly neglected or simply little known in the English-speaking world, are made accessible through new translations and a completely fresh editorial approach. Through these short classic works, each little more than 100 pages in length, the reader will be introduced to the greatest writers from all times and all cultures.

For more information on Hesperus Press, please visit our website: **www.hesperuspress.com**

ET REMOTISSIMA PROPE

SELECTED TITLES FROM HESPERUS PRESS

Author	Title	Foreword writer
Pietro Aretino	*The School of Whoredom*	Paul Bailey
Jane Austen	*Love and Friendship*	Fay Weldon
Honoré de Balzac	*Colonel Chabert*	A.N. Wilson
Charles Baudelaire	*On Wine and Hashish*	Margaret Drabble
Giovanni Boccaccio	*Life of Dante*	A.N. Wilson
Charlotte Brontë	*The Green Dwarf*	Libby Purves
Mikhail Bulgakov	*The Fatal Eggs*	Doris Lessing
Giacomo Casanova	*The Duel*	Tim Parks
Miguel de Cervantes	*The Dialogue of the Dogs*	
Anton Chekhov	*The Story of a Nobody*	Louis de Bernières
Wilkie Collins	*Who Killed Zebedee?*	Martin Jarvis
Arthur Conan Doyle	*The Tragedy of the Korosko*	Tony Robinson
William Congreve	*Incognita*	Peter Ackroyd
Joseph Conrad	*Heart of Darkness*	A.N. Wilson
Gabriele D'Annunzio	*The Book of the Virgins*	Tim Parks
Dante Alighieri	*New Life*	Louis de Bernières
Daniel Defoe	*The King of Pirates*	Peter Ackroyd
Marquis de Sade	*Incest*	Janet Street-Porter
Charles Dickens	*The Haunted House*	Peter Ackroyd
Fyodor Dostoevsky	*Poor People*	Charlotte Hobson
Joseph von Eichendorff	*Life of a Good-for-nothing*	
George Eliot	*Amos Barton*	Matthew Sweet
F. Scott Fitzgerald	*The Rich Boy*	John Updike
Gustave Flaubert	*Memoirs of a Madman*	Germaine Greer
E.M. Forster	*Arctic Summer*	Anita Desai
Ugo Foscolo	*Last Letters of Jacopo Ortis*	Valerio Massimo Manfredi
Elizabeth Gaskell	*Lois the Witch*	Jenny Uglow